Short Story International

Tales by the World's
Great Contemporary Writers
Presented Unabridged

All selections in
Short Story International
are reprinted full and
unabridged in the author's
own words. Nothing is
added, subtracted,
condensed or rewritten.

Editor
Sylvia Tankel

Associate Editor
Erik Sandberg-Diment

Contributing Editor
John Harr

Assistant Editors
Mildred Butterworth
Arlene Loveless
Kirsten Hammerle

Art Director
Mort Rubenstein

Drawings by
John Groth

Circulation Director
Nat Raboy

Production Director
Ludwig K. Marz

Business Manager
John O'Connor

Publisher
Sam Tankel

Volume 3, Number 13, April 1979. *Short Story International* (USPS 375-970) Copyright © by International Cultural Exchange 1979. Printed in the U.S.A. All rights reserved. Reproduction in whole or in part prohibited. Second-class postage paid at Great Neck, N.Y. 11022 and at additional mailing offices. Editorial offices: P.O. Box 405, Great Neck, N.Y. 11022. Enclose stamped, self-addressed envelope with previously published stories submitted for possible reprinting in *Short Story International*. Please note *SSI* does not accept unpublished original manuscripts. One year (six issues) subscription for U.S., U.S. possessions $12, Canada $15, other countries $17. Single copy price $2.50. For subscriptions and address changes write to *Short Story International*, P.O. Box 928, Farmingdale, N.Y. 11737. *Short Story International* is published bimonthly by International Cultural Exchange, 6 Sheffield Road, Great Neck, N.Y. 11021. Postmaster please send Form 3579 to P.O. Box 928, Farmingdale, N.Y. 11737.

Note from the Editor

With this issue, carrying a new cover, *Short Story International* begins its third year.

Despite the long-standing publishers' shibboleth: "Short stories don't sell," we were convinced there is a need, a market, for quality short stories—complete, unabridged stories that bring a rich and intimate experience of the world in which we live.

We share the exhilaration of those who disproved earlier cliches like: "You can't break the sound barrier" and "You'll never get it off the ground." Everyone who has participated in moving SSI from an idea to a growing, healthy reality is jubilant.

The Tower of Babel does not hinder us; readers tell us our story translations are sensitive, often brilliant. We have unwavering faith in SSI as a vehicle to better understanding among people of all lands through the power and magic of short stories by contemporary writers.

You, our readers, have supported our efforts; we invite you to share our sense of accomplishment as we keep circling the globe to bring great short stories from more and more writers and more and more lands to you for your reading pleasure.

Copyrights
and acknowledgments

We wish to express deep thanks to the authors, publishers, translators and literary agents for their permission to reprint the stories in this issue.

"The Traitor" by J.B. Jeffries, reprinted by permission of the author and editor of *Blackwood's Magazine*, Scotland, 1977, in which it first appeared. "The Confession of Elesbão de Castro" from *O Pastor* by Paulo Amador, translation by Thomas Colchie. Copyright 1971 Paulo Amador. "Sleep It Off, Lady" from the book *Sleep It Off, Lady* by Jean Rhys. Copyright © 1976 Jean Rhys. Reprinted by permission of Harper & Row, Publishers, Inc. and Andre Deutsch Ltd. "The Windward Islands" from *My Disappearance in Providence* by Alfred Andersch. English translation copyright © 1977 by Doubleday & Company, Inc. Published by Doubleday & Company, Inc. "The Man on the Gray Horse" by E.G. Chipulina. Reprinted by permission of the author and editor of *Blackwood's Magazine*. "A Case of Immaculate Conception" from *Myself a Mandarin* by Austin Coates. Copyright © 1968 Austin Coates. Reprinted by permission of Heinemann Educational Books (Asia) Ltd. "The Kite-Maker" from *A Girl from Copenhagen* by Ruskin Bond. Copyright © 1977 Ruskin Bond. Published by India Paperbacks. "The Celebrants" from *The Bridal Canopy* by S.Y. Agnon. English translation by I.M. Lask. Copyright © 1967 Schocken Books Inc. Reprinted by permission of Schocken Books Inc. "Catching Up" from *The New Net Goes Fishing* by Witi Ihimaera. Copyright © 1977 Witi Ihimaera. Published by William Heinemann (NZ) Ltd. "The Wheel" by Jose V. Ayala originally appeared in the *Philippines Free Press*. Copyright 1978 Jose V. Ayala. "An Early Frost" by L.W. Michaelson first appeared in *Descant*, 1975. Reprinted by permission of the author and *Descant*. "The Prevaricator" from *The Talismans and Other Stories* by Carlos Baker. Reprinted by permission of Charles Scribner's Sons. Copyright © 1976 Carlos Baker.

Table of Contents

"In the Balkans, they say, a ghost may sometimes carry a long, sharp knife."

The Traitor

BY J.B. JEFFRIES

A chance encounter surfaces a poignant partisan mission.

THIRTY-ODD years, almost half man's allotted span. A longish time, measured laboriously by the day-to-day stresses of life. But a chasm instantly to be bridged by the mind responding to certain stimuli. It was mid-afternoon, I was walking across the square, encapsulated as we all are within the present moment, when there he was—Stanislaus.

Much heavier now; his athlete's body had thickened and expanded, not with fat, one sensed, but with layer upon layer of superfluous muscle. He sat on a marble bench, one massive leg crossed upon the other, feeding from a paper bag a flock of pigeons gathered before him. A truly remarkable figure, bull-necked, grey-headed now; the ageing gladiator, grown stiff in the joints perhaps—but immediately and unmistakably Stanislaus in the flesh, patriot, partisan, brilliant saboteur and friend. Returned from the dead? Impossible.

Stanislaus was his code-name in the underground. We knew him by no other. Too tall, too striking, entirely too memorable. A secret agent should be nondescript, average, capable of losing himself in a crowd. Nevertheless, because in 1942 he was esteemed to be the most competent explosives expert among the by no means incompetent handful of Free Yugoslav volunteers, most of the really difficult targets were assigned to him. In former days those huge hands, now scattering crumbs and birdseed, could handle in the dark the fulminate of mercury and the delicate wiring and mechanism of a demolition-charge with the unerring and exquisite touch of a great artist.

Was this his ghost that I was seeing in the hot broad daylight of an Australian afternoon? As I halted before him the pigeons rose with a clatter and immediately alighted again a few feet to his right, as if seeking in his shadow protection from an intruder. For an instant he remained immobile, gazing up at me. Then it seemed as if a mountain materialized as he came to his feet and towered above me; he was six foot eight tall, if an inch.

"Digger!" In that muted bass voice of his, the greeting rumbled out somewhere above my head, those two great hands descended upon my shoulders, and I was being shaken vigorously. "Where have you been, Digger? Where have you *been*?" (There were only two Australians serving in our Royal Navy flotilla of submarines, a Torpedo Officer and myself. So in our respective ships we were called "Digger.")

For years, perhaps, I had not remembered that dark coastline nor this man who once had clambered down the pressure hull of the submarine into the rubber dinghy. Beneath his shirt he wore two detonators strapped to his chest with surgical tape—to kill himself if he was captured. "My escape route," he called them. Later, when the report of his success followed by the news of his death had filtered back to us, I had mourned him briefly and in private, as one learns to mourn one's friends in war. And afterwards the years went by.

Now in the sunlight, the stream of life itself, our fellow citizens intent upon that illusory moment of Time Present, projected eagerly toward Time Future, flowed ceaselessly past and around us as we stood like two boulders motionless in the flood. Momentarily speechless after the shock of meeting, searching for the words that could bridge the yawning years and recreate for us Time long Past.

After such a lapse of time it should be easy to tell the story without reticence. But old habits die hard. I doubt whether the Official Secrets Act any longer applies. Nevertheless, habits of those days, of silence, of secrecy, were so deeply ingrained that it is still difficult to bring oneself to disclose in print the names of people, of ships, of places, and the dates—even if one remembers them—associated with operations described once upon a time as MOST SECRET. It is ridiculous to be inhibited by those old disciplines. The world has grown older, many of the people concerned may long be dead, and one hopes the old fears and hatreds have vanished with them. Yet one feels the need to practice discretion, even now. In the Balkans, they say, a ghost may sometimes carry a long, sharp knife.

My friendship with Stanislaus had begun—it must have been toward the end of 1942 or the beginning of '43. We were just about to leave harbor for our designated patrol-area, so it would have been during the early hours of a dark Egyptian night when he arrived on board, accompanied by Captain S himself. Two files of Marines followed, carrying several crates and boxes. I am positive not even our C.O. had prior knowledge of Stanislaus's existence. Amended Sailing Orders were handed to the C.O. by Captain S. These orders "required and obliged" him before taking up his patrol to put Stanislaus aboard a fishing vessel that on a certain date and at a precise time would identify herself in a given position off the coast of Yugoslavia. In war every operational order was Top Secret, but this was our first introduction to a cloak-and-dagger job.

Not that there was a cloak concealing a lethal weapon on or about the person of the smiling young giant who had joined us. He was dressed in worn and nondescript civilian clothes, and would have passed for a laborer on holiday. Such was my first impression when, as soon as Captain S had taken his departure, I was summoned by the C.O. and ordered to take charge of our passenger and his gear. When I learned what the crates and boxes contained, I had them struck down into the magazine without delay. There seemed to be sufficient explosive in them to blow up a town. Later we were to learn they were to destroy not a town but a building used as the Nazi H.Q. in the city of—call it Graz. This was made known to us by our C.O., who had been put in the picture by Captain S.

On passage to the rendezvous Stanislaus proved to be an excellent messmate, but he did not discuss with us the details of his mission. We inferred that it was to be a hit-and-run raid because our orders required us, after the lapse of ten days, to be close to a small off-lying islet where, with luck, he would rejoin us for passage back to Alexandria. This entailed taking the submarine into fairly shallow waters dangerously close to an enemy-held coastline, and remaining there on the surface for up to half an hour, not knowing whether Stanislaus was still alive. To us it seemed that the overworked and doubtful element Luck was being stretched to its limit. However, wonderful to relate, rejoin us he did. But it was an angry, brooding Stanislaus who came abroad and made no secret of the complete and tragic failure of the operation ashore.

"There was treachery," he growled. "The Germans were waiting like a cat for a mouse. Somewhere there is a traitor. Somehow soon I find him, by God!"

From what he went on to say it seemed that the raid had been planned in considerable haste, almost at the last moment, following a report that Hitler, dissatisfied with the progress of his troops against the partisans, had sent his loathsome disciple Himmler to shake up the Nazi command-structure in Yugoslavia. It was believed that Himmler would be in Graz on a certain day. The possibility of kidnapping him had been studied, but when this was seen to be beyond the power of the local partisans, it was decided to eliminate him by blowing up the headquarters building after his arrival there. The town of Graz had thus become a target of the very first importance, apparently justifying placing at grave risk one of His Majesty's not too numerous submarines.

Stanislaus's part in the operation was to supply and site the explosives, no light task in the circumstances. The leadership of the group was in the hands of a man who, under the code-name Ludovic, later became famous as one of Tito's most brilliant lieutenants and whose mysterious disappearance, on the eve of Yugoslavia's liberation, was never satisfactorily explained. Stanislaus referred to him not only as an old and trusted companion of his boyhood, but also as a patriot and leader, with whom he had been "in the hills" at the outset of Yugoslavia's resistance to the Germans. It was said that formerly he had been an officer in the Royal Yugoslav Army.

All went well until the day before Himmler was expected. Much work had been done, literally underground. Stanislaus arrived and the demolition-charges were laid and fused. Then, at the very last minute, Ludovic began to hanker after the original plan that had been abandoned because sufficient forces were not available. He had heard rumors of the arrival in the neighborhood of several groups of partisans from the north, and decided on making a quick journey to establish contact with them, taking Stanislaus with him. In the event they had found the rumors were an exaggeration. Only a few men had drifted in, and they were poorly armed. Once and for all the hoped-for kidnapping was out of the question, and the two friends returned to Graz, faced with the ticklish business of regaining their secret hiding-place during the curfew.

The enemy patrols were unusually numerous, Stanislaus said, but nevertheless they succeeded in getting within a block of their destination. Then: "Out from a doorway pops this little girl, only a child, and says, 'Stop, patriots! They are waiting for you.' "

It was the truth. Everything had been "blown."

Evidently the identities and whereabouts of every member of the group had been known to the Germans for some time and, Stanislaus believed, all but he and Ludovic were shot or captured, trapped in their supposedly safe hiding-places earlier that evening. And that was the tragic end of "Operation Extractor"—for as such it has been named. In retrospect, it seems at first glance that Allied Intelligence had been surprisingly naïve. Surely the bosses of the Nazi Party would not have planned their itineraries weeks in advance. Yet, paradoxically, the report must have been accurate because Himmler, or someone "fronting" for him, did arrive in Graz on the expected day. Again, if the Germans had set up the visit deliberately to flush out those few members of the Resistance, why, knowing or anticipating our reaction, had our submarine not been detected and attacked on the two occasions we had surfaced almost under their noses? At the time we were content to attribute Stanislaus's escape and our own immunity to that unpredictable factor, Luck. Thirty-odd years were to pass before I learned that Luck was only partially responsible.

Luck, and the inefficiency of an E-boat commander near the Strait of Otranto, certainly accounted for our survival when we went to get Stanislaus out. German or Italian—we did not tarry to discover—the E-boat had rounded the northern point of land that sheltered the tiny bay where, we hoped, Stanislaus had beached and concealed his rubber dinghy. We were under way and diving. The intervening reef had masked the hydrophone effect of the enemy's motors until the enemy was almost on top of us.

O memory, memory! Recalling that moment, I can see and sense everyone in the control-room suddenly frozen, absolutely still, utterly silent. A hand reaching toward a circuit-breaker stopped in mid-reach, the fingers outstretched like a claw. A group of men turned suddenly as if to marble. And yes, even now, I feel my own heart falter and seem to stop; the clang of a depth-charge striking the pressure hull will assuredly be the last sound I shall ever hear. For me, for all of us, the last sound in the world. Then comes physical numbness as the adrenalin begins its merciful task.

Afterwards we laughed heartily at and with the Navigator, who had bitten clean through a pencil that happened to be between his teeth. In fact we laughed heartily at everything and nothing—afterwards. Evidently the enemy had been caught as much by surprise as we had been, and had failed to prime and set his pattern of depth-charges before firing them. And, Luck again, it must have been his last remaining pattern. Although for a time we heard him dashing about above us, keeping contact, no more depth-charges were fired until half an hour later, when one of the consorts he had evidently summoned carried out several noisy attacks on what must have been a ghost echo, well astern of us.

Ghost echoes from the past. Surely this man must be a ghost also. But the deep, excited tones of Stanislaus's voice were decidedly not those of a disembodied spirit. Nor was the grip of his hand on my shoulder that of an astral body. Time Past was merging again with Time Present, and he was saying, "I thought you must all have died. Don't you remember?" Did I not? "There I was. Already I was getting into the little cave when he come round the point. Bang! Bang!"

It would have been the E-boat's mortars throwing the unarmed depth-charges that he had heard. But before I could explain, he was off again.

"I thought you was all kaput. But where have you since been? When I come to Australia I ask. Everywhere, just in case. But you are nowhere."

Where had we both been, if not in Limbo? It was a searching question. At that instant I felt that I had been nowhere, done nothing, since those days when each moment of life and action had in it the unique and moving significance imparted by the conviction that it might be one's last. Clearly this was a question that could not be answered properly in five minutes. Moreover, I had a business appointment, an important one, and was already over five minutes late for it. It was necessary to be very firm. I took him by the arm, a tug moving Leviathan out into the stream, and urged him across the square. The pigeons were forgotten, and it was agreed that he would wait for me. And afterwards. . . .

"Afterwards," he said, "you come with me. I got things to show you."

And show me he did. He took me to a nearby thoroughfare where between the towering blocks of modern, and mostly empty, offices stood the gaping shell of a smaller, older and more gracious building. High above it the jib of a crane was lowering a grabful of rubble into a waiting truck in the street below. Dust and the din of jack-hammers rose from behind the safety-hoardings. As we drew nearer, Stanislaus drew my attention to a large sign masking the sightless eyes of the first-floor windows.

"Stan the Wrecker is here" it proclaimed in letters a yard high.

He waved his arm in a sweeping gesture that almost knocked my hat off.

"You see?" he said. "I am back to my old trade."

This proved to be only one of three major demolitions that his firm, the firm he had founded, was currently engaged in.

"A bloody damn pity," he growled. "The council won't let me blow them. Too much risk to windows and other foundations, they say. But if only they let me use a few little charges in the right places. Poof! down she would come—as gentle as a pack of cards. No worries to anyone. But never mind, I get paid for it just the same."

His enthusiasm and pride in displaying the empire he had created were touching, for he seemed to imply that in some remote way I had been responsible for setting him upon the road to Australia and success. And perhaps during the short-lived period of our old acquaintanceship, I may have waxed eloquent on the subject of Australia, its vastness, its freedom, its challenge and—above all—its contrast to the tortured Europe that seemed then to be exploding in our faces. In the end, when the stateless patriot and fighter for freedom had to choose a country of adoption, he had remembered.

"First I am a New Australian," he said. "Now I am an old one. Too damn old sometimes. But how do you like that? Dinkum Aussie, eh?"

He had stopped outside a mini-skyscraper and was pointing to the name of a firm among the list of tenants. I read "Stan S. Laws & Co. Pty Ltd, Demolitions." Shortly afterwards he was ushering me through a door marked "Managing Director," and was offering me the choice of slivovitz, whisky, beer or rum.

During the next half-hour we exchanged our post-war stories. He spoke of his experiences as a fencing contractor out back, as a shearer, as a miner at Broken Hill, then as a builder, and finally as a demolisher of buildings. He had married his wife, Rosie, at Broken Hill. Their son was an art student and still single. Their daughter—"I got a pigeon-pair"—had married an airline pilot, and Stanislaus had recently become a grandfather—"One little boy."

By the end of this exchange the brooding outline of that old, dark coast had receded and grown dim, remaining merely as a nebulous shadow on the far horizon of my mind. Finally, his secretary came into the room with a tray of papers to be signed, and I stood up to take my leave.

"Just a minute," demanded Stan S. Laws, the Managing Director. "Where you think you're going?" He knew by now that I was only passing through the city and was alone. "You're coming home with me. I got to show you to Rosie."

And so it came about that, long after nightfall on that long, hot, midsummer day, Stanislaus and I were sitting in the semi-darkness of a wide veranda overlooking the little inlet whose foreshore formed the eastern boundary of his garden.

His son, Ludovic, had left us soon after dinner to attend what he described as a "turn" and dear, kind little Rosie, who looked far too young to be a grandmother, had sat with us for a time and then gone to bed. Stanislaus had promised to drive me to the local station, where there was a train service to the city—"When I finish this cigar, maybe." He had been telling me about his and Rosie's travels with their family over the past five years, after the twins had left school. They had been to the United States to study new developments in the demolishing and building of cities. Then to Singapore, Hong Kong, Japan and Britain.

"And Europe?" I asked. "Yugoslavia—have you been back there?" I was careful not to say "your own country," for he had adopted Australia whole-heartedly, even aggressively, as his own.

"No," he replied after a pause. "Never." There was another short silence. The tip of his cigar glowed and waned as he drew on it meditatively. "Is strange how that one German could manage to turn a whole continent into beasts, and all so damn quick and sudden. No! Not real beasts," he went on, stroking with one foot the Irish setter lying asleep between us. "Beasts are not cruel, like men are. Beasts defend their own territory. Beasts fight, but not often kill one another except from hunger. Beasts don't torture, corrupt and prevent one another, starve one another and mass-murder one another as those people under that leader did. Fight-

17

ing them, we had to become like them almost. Kill, kill, kill."

"No," he said, after another silence, "I never go back. Too much blood on my hands for that. Already I went back once too often."

"To find a traitor," I prompted him. "Did you find him?"

He made no immediate reply, and I thought he would ignore my question. Then he said softly, "Yes, I did find him. But never I tell anyone, not even Rosie."

He fell silent again and seemed to be listening to the sounds of the night—the miniature crash of wavelets that the waning nor'-easter flung upon the beach, the stirring and rustling of leaves and, farther out in the bay, the muted claging of steel halyards within the metal mast of a moored yacht.

Stanislaus spoke again, as it were at a tangent. "Funny, our meeting today. Two old ghosts. And you leave the country again tomorrow, you said. Maybe you vanish for another thirty years, eh? What was that poetry you said at dinner?"

" 'And I go forever and come again no more,' " I replied, quoting a line of Stevenson.

"That's good. I like it. Well! Maybe I ought to tell someone, someday. Put it on the record?"

"There's not the slightest need, unless you want to." His hesitation was obvious, and the last thing I wished was to pry into his private memories. "I was merely being inquisitive," I added, apologizing. "But when we learned you had blown up that bridge, and later heard the rumor that you had died doing it, for years I used to wonder if the traitor you spoke of had found you before you found him. A ridiculous question, anyhow. Forget it," I said lamely.

To my surprise, he responded readily. "Ah! she was a good one, that bridge. And if the bullet had been a little bit more to the right, I'd have died there, sure enough. But you remember that other operation? What did they call it? 'Extractor.' Silly damn name. Much too many people knew about that one. There was the crew of your boat that met me. There was the people I met after I landed. Too many people all the time. What did we want with all those people? Somewhere among them must be the traitor, but where? So next time I go back I am alone, remember? Only me, Stanislaus. No one ashore knows I am coming, or what I plan to do. In Cairo they said there was this bridge they wanted taken out, so I said 'All right! I take it out for you, one hand, kneeling, only leave me by myself. No signals. Nothing.' "

"What was the set-up?" I asked.

"Single-track railway bridge. Out of a cutting, across a river, through a siding, into another cutting. But high. About sixty feet above the river and maybe two hundred, two-fifty feet long—I forget. Single span, suspension. I had to climb at night to fix the charges. Guards on both sides and dogs—you can imagine."

"No," I said, "I can't imagine how you could manage without a company of men."

Stanislaus shook his head. "No need. Only a very weak guard, about platoon strength, mostly old men and boys. Active enough by day. But at night, except for a sentry on each side, they mostly stay in the hut and leave it to the dogs to give warning. Lucky I always get on well with animals, specially dogs. You ask old Dave Allen here," he said, scratching the Irish setter with the toe of his shoe. "For three nights I sneak in with food. Got them used to my smell. Them fools kept them half-starved, anyhow, so that part was easy. And I could climb all right in the dark, those days. Only getting away afterwards I got a bullet in my shoulder. Lucky not my leg."

"Where did you go?" I asked, already in my mind's eye seeing the enormous fugitive twisting and dodging among boulders on an exposed hillside, outlined by the stars and pursued by streams of tracer-bullets.

"They had a trolley for patrolling their section of the line. Lucky for me it was left unguarded in the excitement. Grade goes down-hill all the way just there for maybe two miles, so I just let her go. After about a mile, I threw myself off and took to the woods. Not difficult then. You see, it was raining. Dogs don't follow scent too good in the rain."

He spoke offhandedly, as if the whole thing, the successful sabotage and all that had led up to it, and the wound and his remarkable escape, had been simply routine. I asked him about the wound in his shoulder.

He made little of it. "Nearly a miss. Pretty good now. Only still I can't lift my left arm high with any weight. Didn't hit any bones or artery, just ripped the muscle to pieces pretty bad. But bled a lot. Lucky I got over the top into the next valley before I passed out."

"How far had you gone?"

"Oh! long time ago. Don't remember that part too good, now. Not far. Maybe five, six mile—I forget. Anyhow they found me there in the morning, a couple of partisans. There was a mine pretty close. Not worked any more for years. That's where they carried me. Later an old woman come and cleaned me. Gave me soup. She seemed oh! so old then, but maybe not so old as me now. Funny! I don't feel old yet. They was all half-starved, the people, but always she brought me something to eat. Put cobwebs on my shoulder. How do you like that? Just cobwebs, but they healed it quick. No poison. When I got little bit strong, I left there—I was lucky."

"Lucky!" I echoed. "But where did you go?"

"You remember Ludovic? Well, I went to where I reckoned I would find him sooner or later. Not far. Only forty, fifty miles from where I was. All my own country—you understand? Where we was born, Ludovic and me. Know it like I know my hand." He raised his right hand, holding the smouldering cigar, and let it fall again. "Still pretty weak, I was. Good deal of pain. Damn hungry too. But I made it."

He lapsed into silence, and when he resumed his tone was no longer offhand and matter-of-fact. Clearly he was under the spell of a memory that was dear to him.

"Only a little place. What we call a summer farm, high up on a shelf in the mountains. But no animals there now, only the pigeons in the loft. Everyone gone. Little fields, all growing wild flowers, not crops. German aircraft fly over every day, but I stay out of sight. Not light fire until nightfall. No smoke. It was summer then. You remember?"

He seemed to be speaking not to me, but to someone who had shared his isolation. Nevertheless I murmured, "I remember." I doubt if he heard me.

"There was an old grape-vine there, thick as a mat. I got grapes here too, but not as sweet." He made a gesture at the far corner of the veranda where a vine formed a heavy curtain of leaves. "I sit under that vine and sleep and drink and feed the pigeons while Jerry flies over. Safe as this. Oh! for days and days. In the end, sure enough, Ludovic come, late at night. Very surprised to find me there, you understand. Though he was partisan chief for all that area, no one tell him I come back. No signals from Cairo, remember?" Manifestly, Stanislaus was pleased by the recollection. He continued, "That was because I see no one, talk to no one, this time, except the old woman and the freedom-fighters who hid me in the mine."

"But you wanted to see Ludovic," I said. "How did you know he would come?"

"His farm," he replied. "Once much land, now is the only thing he has left. I knew he would come, even if only to feed the pigeons, and to feel safe for a little while. Oh! very bad times, he told me. Nazis shot many hostages, because of the bridge, and they are pushing his group very hard. Ludovic told me, ordered me, to stay up there until I was strong again. Still too weak, he reckoned. Only get in the way.

"Long days, those," he went on softly. "Like when I was a little boy on holiday. Long days. And the hills where him and me run as children, the hills across the big, deep valley, blue in the distance. Like the mountains of a dream. Everything so silent. And I remember a lot of childhood things, silly things, and try not to think of what they are doing to my people and my country, everywhere. Waiting only to get strong again so that I can go down again and kill, kill, kill."

He got up from his chair and refilled with peach brandy the two glasses that stood on the table between us.

"You still want to hear all this, Digger?" he asked, attempting to appear casual. "Maybe I talk too much. Old men do."

"No," I replied, "please go on. After all, I did have a share in your being there."

He nodded and, taking his glass with him, went to sit sideways on the broad stone coping of the wall that formed a curving balustrade on that part of the veranda. His face was half turned towards the garden, away from me and the dim, shaded lamp standing behind the chairs. When he spoke again it seemed that he was talking not so much to me as to the night, the timeless night of the past, and to the familiar spirits who peopled it for him.

"So," he said, in a low voice carrying deep undertones of sadness. He was now talking, in memory, to Ludovic. "There you were at last, my old, old *suradnik*. All these years I never tell it to a soul. No one. You remember the pigeons? There was some grain I used to give them in the evenings. So greedy they was, so tame. And the squabs was all there was to eat. Already I had found the transceiver. German, but nothing in that. Just about the only equipment we had at that time was what we captured from the Nazis. No, so far everything still O.K.

"But that evening you come early, remember? First time you come early, in daylight. Remember? We sat there, talking and drinking, pigeons all round our feet, pecking at the grain. So peaceful, just like old times. And then I see this bird among them—very tired, very hungry. A homer, with the little canister on his leg.

"And as I reach for him, to take him, you make a noise to frighten them away, but not soon enough, just not soon enough. Oh! why were you so slow? So tired you must have been. Tired out, just like the bird. So far to come, so much to carry on your mind, so much twisting and dodging, so many enemies all the way. Where to turn next? Where to hide? But you must come home.

"He could have shot me," Stanislaus continued turning his face slightly towards me. "You see, I was holding the bird in both hands. No need to look at what was in the little canister. Just to look at Ludovic's face. And he was a brave man, the bravest. Don't I know? Children together. And together in the hills afterwards, when he come back, hunting and hunted—both. Braver than me, I tell you. But now, at last, he is broken. After a while we talk, and he tells me everything that has happened.

"Well! Four, five months before this time, the Nazis take prisoner his wife. She was with the partisans too. Big, strong, very beautiful girl. I knew her also, since she was very young. At first Ludovic don't know what happen to her. Then he thinks maybe she has died, been killed. He can't find out. All this until this S.S. bastard,

Stompitz, sends him a message. She is still alive, in fact she has not been harmed, he says. But to keep her that way, Ludovic must 'co-operate.' " Stanislaus paused to clear his throat and spit into the night. "Clever bastards. Then Stompitz sets out the plan for that phoney operation at Graz—the mock raid—to impress Himmler, of course. And at the end this Stompitz says Ludovic's wife will be in the cells at Graz, in case Ludovic decides to play it for real. Plain enough now; they could have taken Ludovic as well as the others, but better to keep him going as a perpetual traitor, under threat.

" 'What would you have done?' Ludovic asks me. I am afraid to answer. . . .

"So Ludovic was lost. Everything happened in Graz that night just like I told you. Only he took me away with him to escape the capture and the killing. He never warned the Nazis about the submarine, either. To save me.

"And then, remembering all this, suddenly I know another terrible thing—just as if he had told me. He is doing it again. All those men, his command, he has left in the jaws of a trap. I know it. That is why he order me to stay—to save me again. That is why he come up early to the farm, not at night as always before. To send or receive a message. I don't know; maybe they promise to release her this time, let her go. One woman for two, three hundred lives. It could be. And I look at the message the pigeon brought. No words, only figures. Code. No matter that I can't read it; Ludovic knew that I knew. Always we were like that. As boys we were like two little dogs. You know, a look, a movement of the head, we knew what the other was thinking.

"So now he says, 'All right, I go back. Maybe there is still time. If not, better I die there too.' "

Stanislaus's back was turned to me now, and he was speaking again to the night in tones so low that I had difficulty in following what he said. And again he was addressing, not me, but the fallen idol of his youth.

"But how can I trust you now? I do not know you any more like I did. Trust you with my life—yes! And anyhow I don't matter any more. But all those other lives, how about them?"

Stanislaus suddenly turned his old gladiator's face toward me.

"Only one thing to do then. I stand up and begin taking off my clothes, undressing. But Ludovic don't move, just sits there staring across the valley like he is turned to stone. Not moving. And finally I have to start unbuttoning his jacket for him, like he was still very young child. And suddenly I am so angry that I slap his face; that too, as if he were only little boy. But in the end it was done and there we was—Ludovic wearing my clothes, me in his sort of uniform. I take everything of his and give him all of mine. Swap. He has all my false identity-papers, everything. Last of all I hand him my knife and my pistol, safety off. And I tell him—if he wants to live—where to go, what to say to be taken care of. But it is like he has stopped living already. Says nothing. Don't even look at me. Oh! my poor Ludovic.

"In the end I turned my back on him and went away. Soon I must hurry, hurry, but first I must give him his chance and I walk slow and straight. Last thing of all, where the path goes down out of sight, I looked back. Still he has not moved from his seat under the old grape-vine near the door."

Stanislaus paused and for a time seemed intent on the attenuated cubes of ice that remained, half afloat, in his glass. At last the nor'-easter had died away and from the garden the chorus of night insects seemed unusually shrill. I was wondering what I could say to ease the tension, when he spoke again.

"Already I am far down the mountain when I think I hear the sound of the shot, very faint. Seems I can feel the bitter taste of the muzzle in my mouth and the bullet bursting my own brain. Then I know he is dead."

I left my chair and together we stood for a time in the silence at the veranda's edge, looking into the semi-darkness where the sleeping surface of the bay reflected the crescent of a waning moon, not long risen.

After a time Stanislaus made some business of relighting the stump of his cigar with a hand that was laudably steady. Then: "No stopping," he said softly. "No going back. No dying, even. Too many lives at stake. Nearly three hundred."

Apparently the partisans, usually operating in small, highly mobile groups over a wide area, had been massed on the pretext of attacking a village and road junction held by the enemy. They were to be surrounded and annihilated at dawn by a German force that was moving into position during the night.

"You were in time?" I asked.

"Only just. Lucky I knew where the H.Q. was. Couldn't reach a few outposts, but most got out O.K.—fighting."

I could imagine the desperate withdrawal of the men of that small force, who had been betrayed by their leader and saved at the very last moment by Stanislaus, almost literally hurling himself down the mountain to their rescue.

"How did they react afterwards, the partisans?" I asked. "I mean when they learned Ludovic had been a traitor."

"How would they learn that?" said Stanislaus sharply. "Why should I tell them? Never I told anyone till I told you here, tonight. Don't you see? It was the body of Stanislaus, the dynamite man, that the Germans find later at the farm. Everything there to prove it. For the partisans, it was me who was Ludovic. I had all his papers. Everything of his. No disgrace, no worries at all. Not even with Tito."

I was astounded. What sort of Balkan fairy tale was this? The face, the form, the voice, the mannerisms of Ludovic, even his pattern of thinking must have been perfectly familiar to his staff and his troops. One cannot assume another's identity simply by wearing his clothes and carrying his personal papers. How then could I be expected to believe that an impersonation such as he claimed could be carried out and sustained by Stanislaus who was physically unique, a giant of a man? This was expecting me to believe the incredible and I said as much.

For a time Stanislaus gave no indication of having heard me. He turned away, and after grinding out the butt of his cigar in an ashtray, flung it with a wide sweep of the arm as in years gone by he would have flung a hand-grenade, far out toward the water. When finally he spoke it was almost in a whisper.

"Even now it hurts to tell," he said, "that Ludovic was my brother. We was identical twins."

J.B. Jeffries is a pen-name. A fourth-generation Australian, the author is a farmer, sailor, private pilot and glider pilot.

"And you, Carmelita, only you still perservere, there in the window, tempting little boys."

The Confession of Elesbão de Castro

BY PAULO AMADOR

A young seminarian faces his frailties.

—DON'T you want a lollipop, Elesbão de Castro?

—No, I'll never take one of your lollipops.

—Would you shun my enchantments then, Elesbão de Castro?

—Yes, Carmelita, I would shun all of your diabolical temptations because I know you're a witch and you've already carried five lovers off to your bed of perdition.

—I? But I of all people, . . . Elesbão de Castro?

—Yes, you, Carmelita.

—But look how you've made me cry, Elesbão de Castro.

Oh, Carmelita, you may cry but you'll never manage to move the hearts of the townspeople. They saw you return from the camp of the Gypsies. And you brought back a green poison on your lips and a silver wand in your hand. The poison, perfidious creature, you used to prepare those lollipops with which you always entice little boys so you can carry them off with you to your sinful bed. The silver wand, in your wickedness, you set into the clay jug from which you always drink. That's what keeps you eternal. Eternal? Yes, because the years pass, the boys grow old and their grandchildren marry. And you, Carmelita, only you still perservere, there in the window, tempting little boys.

—Don't you want a lollipop, child of God?

Why is it they've never apprehended you? Because you keep a long cord and on it are the knots of the lives of each and every grown-up in the town. When you untie a knot, someone dies, and you sit there in your window watching the funeral and everybody stares at your face. But no one dares to confront you, Carmelita, since it still remains for you to unravel those knots in the lives of Brejolândia.

—You must urinate into this, Elesbão de Castro.

—I already made peepee. I don't have anymore. I can't anymore.

—Oh, but you can, you just have to want to. You must, Elesbão de Castro.

—But I really can't. I already did all I could down to the last drop of peepee.

—You can do a little more, Elesbão de Castro. You just need to urinate right into here. You're passing albumin. You can't eat any more eggs.

—But I don't want to eat any more eggs.

—You need to eat eggs, Elesbão de Castro. Egg has calcium, you're a growing boy, your organism might be losing precious nutrients.

How long did it last? I don't really know. But I don't manage to pee. I strain very hard. The test tube shakes in my fingers. Then finally, I manage. And now I'm certain of it. He is a sorcerer, just like Carmelita. She ran off the day that the constable threatened her saying: "Enough of your witchcraft or you're going straight to jail, Carmelita." She actually tried to insist she wasn't a witch. But the constable too had once been a boy. "I'm such an old woman, constable. Please, sir, you wouldn't have me arrested, would you?" But the constable was a strong-minded person, stronger than Carmelita's enchantments, and he said: "The law has no age. According to the constitution, everyone is equal before the law, including old crones and wizards." Carmelita fled.

—Excellent, Elesbão de Castro. There's nothing in your urine. You may continue to eat eggs.

—But I don't like eggs.

—You must eat them just the same, Elesbão de Castro. Egg gives you sustenance, it's good for the health. You need to have strong bones. You lose a great deal indulging in those nocturnal pollutions.

—But I said already, I haven't indulged in any nocturnal pollutions. I've just made peepee in my bed.

—That's simply because you pay no attention. I'm certain you've been indulging yourself in all sorts of nocturnal pollutions.

Why do they allow madmen to wander about so freely here? Why this terrible presence. He called me, and I came. He said he needed help, and I helped him. Back in Brejolândia madmen always get locked up in jail. They stay there waiting until such time as they forget they are mad and return to normal. The cell is guarded by two soldiers. If one of them leaves, he has to ring a bell three times to call the other. The madmen are never to be left alone. They can't be. They may climb up on the roof and stand there engaging in all sorts of unseemly behavior. One of them once threw the roofing tiles down at the street below; another took out his private, waving it at your girls and saying: "You're the ones who know alright;" a third was even naked, saying that the end of the world had come. He wanted to dive off the roof into the street, saying that the tide was rising and Noah was already close at hand.

—You received my note, Elesbão de Castro.

—Yes, Father. I just got it this minute, and came running.

—I was afraid that you might choose not to come. I need your help.

—Afraid I might not come? But why not, Father?

—Come now, Elesbão de Castro. All the boys are afraid of me.

—Honestly, Father. I never knew anything about that.

—It's obvious they are, Elesbão. Every one of them is frightened of me. I can sense it when I'm with you all at recess. There now, the rector is shaving his tonsure. But look how the boys crowd around the rector. That never happens with me. They never crowd around me.

—Yes they do, Father. You just haven't noticed.

—Elesbão de Castro, let's you and I be frank with each other. Why are all the boys so frightened of me?

—Maybe because you go down into the catacombs, sir.

—Come now, Elesbão, I go there simply out of duty. I had to gather up the bones and skull of our rector, the deceased ex-rector. The only thing down there is death, that's all. And what is death to a seminarian? You're not about to tell me that you boys are afraid of death.

—Then, I don't know, sir, perhaps because you're a psychologist. Everybody's afraid of psychologists. You can always guess everything. So they're afraid. You always guess, Father, but you don't say what.

—Frankly, Elesbão . . . No joking with me now. Do you know what a psychologist is?

—Psychology is the part of philosophy which studies the psyche, the spirit, the soul, its reactions, its impulses, the intrinsic causality of human actions.

The night before the boys were out hunting lightning bugs in the pasture and they climbed up into the plum trees to get a look at the world. They saw the girls who live on the other side of the wall change their clothes, without closing the window curtains. Elesbão wanted to climb too, but he didn't. Right now the psychologist is standing there in front of him. Will he manage to guess, with those eyes of his, how much you longed to climb up into those trees? Elesbão squeezed the "Vade Mecum" in his pocket. Inside, on a blank page, is written "Ad Usum Elesbão de Castro." The highest marks in penmanship. That fine, elongated lettering, like his grandfather's or the solemn annotations and signatures of the ancient Fathers in the books of the library.

—Alright, Elesbão de Castro. You can relax now.

—But I'm not tense.

—Come now, listen to you . . . Are you trying to tell me that you're not afraid?

With his back turned, leaning over his laboratory instruments, he looks just like some specter at Carnival that cavorts happily through the streets of Brejolândia, singing, dancing, frightening the children. It doesn't help to try to run. Far too many specters are always singing away until Ash Wednesday.

That's right. Elesbão de Castro. I do know everything. I'm like those specters of Brejolândia or like some serpent who attracts the frog in order to eat him. Only by eliminating me, Elesbão de Castro, the way one gets rid of a snake by using a shotgun, or tears off all the masks and costumes of the specters . . . Because now you know that the specters are make-believe and none of them come out of the grave in order to dance at Carnival. The dead only wish to rest in peace, Elesbão de Castro. The most they can manage is a slight procession, during Lent at midnight.

—What's this, Elesbão? Afraid of me?

—Who are you, demon from hell?

—I'm your uncle, Elesbão. Your uncle Zé. Want to see? I'll take off the mask.

—Go to the devil, my uncle doesn't wear a skeleton.

The angel on the cover of the book laughs at Elesbão. The priest says:

—I just remembered, I have to go to the chapel a moment. I'll be right back, Elesbão.

At the corner of the bed is the skull of the ex-rector. Dry, on top of the night table, ribs strewn on the floor like dirty laundry, eye sockets empty, the teeth repaired a while back by the Father dentist. Brejolândia should be here. There, they still argued whether the skull of a man was the same as an ox's or whether a woman's was the same as a nanny goat's. It didn't matter if the doctor exhibited a model skeleton at a cockfight or over at the Alaska Bar, a diagram of a skeleton, showing how the white part was what we're like inside. He had studied all that in a university somewhere. If he only had some money he would have a skeleton sent all the way from Belo Horizonte just to prove what he was saying. The doctor began drinking out of disgust. No one believed him. One day a peddler arrived saying that rheumatism can attack one hundred and eight bones in the apparatus of the human anatomy, tarsus, metatarsus, finger, phalanx, middle phalanx, terminal phalanx, and that everything the doctor had told them about the skeleton was the gospel truth, but that the cure for any ills was in the little yellow vial wrapped in yellowed cellophane that he was selling for five hundred a bottle and three for a thousand. The doctor was ecstatic. He went over to the plaza personally to recommend the peddler's curative. Arm and arm together, the two of them sold little phials of electric eel oil, genuine eel oil from the Amazon.

—Elesbão, confess your sins.

—I've indulged in nocturnal pollutions.

—That isn't a sin, my son.

—I've had bad thoughts.

—Did you consent to them?

—Yes, Father.

—Then confess to God.

—Many times I lacked charity, Father.

—When, Elesbão? How do you lack charity?

—I wished bad things for people, Father.

The priest placed his hand gently upon Elesbão's head.

—Come now, Elesbão de Castro, God forgives all that. Such is only human.

—But I wished bad things on people who are kind.

—No, my son, your heart is still too young to wish ill upon those who are good.

—But it's true, Father.

—Go in peace, my son, and when you leave, close the door behind you.

—I still have another sin, Father.

—Tell me, Elesbão de Castro.

—I had a love, Father. Before coming to the seminary. I never told it in confession.

—Children's games. Elesbão de Castro.

—No, Father, we consummated the act.

—Children's games, Elesbão de Castro.

—But I still have thoughts about her, Father.

—About whom, Elesbão?

—Carmelita.

—Carmelita?
—Yes, Carmelita.
—A beautiful name.
—Is it a sacrilege?
—It's no more than a sin.
—And will God forgive me?
—Now, now, my son, God too was once a boy.

Paulo Amador was born December 1944 in Diamantina, Minas Gerais, Brazil. He studied at a Catholic seminary, but eventually decided not to become a priest, took a law degree and became a professional journalist. O Pastor, a collection of short stories, won the 1971 Union of Brazilian Writers' fiction prize. Mr. Amador has published other short story collections and a novel. Thomas Colchie, his translator, has been interested in languages and translating since childhood. Mr. Colchie is well-known to Latin American authors.

"She stopped herself from saying:
'I can't because I'm afraid.' "

Sleep It Off, Lady

BY JEAN RHYS

An engrossing, unsettling story skillfully developed.

ONE October afternoon Mrs. Baker was having tea with Miss Verney and talking about the proposed broiler factory in the middle of the village where they both lived. Miss Verney, who had not been listening attentively, said, "You know Letty, I've been thinking a great deal about death lately. I hardly ever do, strangely enough."

"No dear," said Mrs. Baker. "It isn't strange at all. It's quite natural. We old people are rather like children, we live in the present as a rule. A merciful dispensation of providence."

"Perhaps," said Miss Verney doubtfully.

Mrs. Baker said "we old people" quite kindly, but could not help knowing that while she herself was only sixty-three and might, with any luck, see many a summer (after many a summer dies the swan, as some man said), Miss Verney, certainly well over seventy, could hardly hope for anything of the sort. Mrs. Baker gripped the arms of her chair. "Many a summer, touch wood and please God," she thought. Then she remarked that it was getting dark so early now and wasn't it extraordinary how time flew.

Miss Verney listened to the sound of the car driving away, went back to her sitting-room and looked out of the window at the flat fields, the apple trees, the lilac tree that wouldn't flower again, not for ten years they told her, because lilacs won't stand being pruned. In the distance there was a rise in the ground—you could hardly call it a hill—and three trees so exactly shaped and spaced that they looked artificial. "It would be rather lovely covered in snow," Miss Verney thought. "The snow, so white, so smooth and in the end so boring. Even the hateful shed wouldn't look so bad." But she'd made up her mind to forget the shed.

Miss Verney had decided that it was an eyesore when she came to live in the cottage. Most of the paint had worn off the once-black galvanized iron. Now it was a greenish color. Part of the roof was loose and flapped noisily in windy weather and a small gate off its hinges leaned up against the entrance. Inside it was astonishingly large, the far end almost dark. "What a waste of space," Miss Verney thought. "That must come down." Strange that she hadn't noticed it before.

Nails festooned with rags protruded from the only wooden rafter. There was a tin bucket with a hole, a huge dustbin. Nettles flourished in one corner but it was the opposite corner which disturbed her. Here was piled a rusty lawnmower, an old chair with a carpet draped over it, several sacks, and the remains of what had once been a bundle of hay. She found herself imagining that a fierce and dangerous animal lived there and called aloud: "Come out, come out, Shredni Vashtar, the beautiful." Then rather alarmed at herself she walked away as quickly as she could.

But she was not unduly worried. The local builder had done several odd jobs for her when she moved in and she would speak to him when she saw him next.

"Want the shed down?" said the builder.

"Yes," said Miss Verney. "It's hideous, and it takes up so much space."

"It's on the large side," the builder said.

"Enormous. Whatever did they use it for?"

"I expect it was the garden shed."

"I don't care what it was," said Miss Verney. "I want it out of the way."

The builder said that he couldn't manage the next week, but the Monday after that he'd look in and see what could be done. Monday came and Miss Verney waited but he didn't arrive. When this had happened twice she realized that he didn't mean to come and wrote to a firm in the nearest town.

A few days later a cheerful young man knocked at the door, explained who he was and asked if she would let him know exactly what she wanted. Miss Verney, who wasn't feeling at all well, pointed, "I want that pulled down. Can you do it?"

The young man inspected the shed, walked round it, then stood looking at it.

"I want it destroyed," said Miss Verney passionately, "utterly destroyed and carted away. I hate the sight of it."

"Quite a job," he said candidly.

And Miss Verney saw what he meant. Long after she was dead and her cottage had vanished it would survive. The tin bucket and the rusty lawnmower, the pieces of rag fluttering in the wind. All would last forever.

Eyeing her rather nervously he became businesslike. "I see what you want, and of course we can let you have an estimate of the cost. But you realize that if you pull the shed down you take away from the value of your cottage?"

"Why?" said Miss Verney.

"Well," he said, "very few people would live here without a car. It could be converted into a garage easily or even used as it is. You can decide of course when you have the estimate whether you think it worth the expense and . . . the trouble. Good day."

Left alone, Miss Verney felt so old, lonely and helpless that she began to cry. No builder would tackle that shed, not for any price she could afford. But crying relieved her and she soon felt quite cheerful again. It was ridiculous to brood, she told herself. She quite liked the cottage. One morning she'd wake up and know what to do about the shed, meanwhile she wouldn't look at the thing. She wouldn't think about it.

But it was astonishing how it haunted her dreams. One night she was standing looking at it changing its shape and becoming a very smart, shiny, dark blue coffin picked out in white. It reminded her of a dress she had once worn. A voice behind her said: "That's the laundry."

"Then oughtn't I to put it away?" said Miss Verney in her dream.

"Not just yet. Soon," said the voice so loudly that she woke up.

She had dragged the large dustbin to the entrance and, because it was too heavy for her to lift, had arranged for it to be carried to the gate every week for the dustmen to collect. Every morning she took a small yellow bin from under the sink and emptied it into the large dustbin, quickly, without lingering or looking around. But on one particular morning the usual cold wind had dropped and she stood wondering if a coat of white paint would improve matters. Paint might look a lot worse, besides who could she get to do it? Then she saw a cat, as she thought, walking slowly across the far end. The sun shone through a chink in the wall. It was a large rat. Horrified, she watched it disappear under the old chair, dropped the yellow bin, walked as fast as she was able up the road and knocked at the door of a shabby thatched cottage.

"Oh Tom. There are rats in my shed. I've just seen a huge one. I'm so desperately afraid of them. What shall I do?"

When she left Tom's cottage she was still shaken, but calmer. Tom had assured her that he had an infallible rat poison, arrangements had been made, his wife had supplied a strong cup of tea.

He came that same day to put down the poison, and when afterwards he rapped loudly on the door and shouted: "Everything under control?" she answered quite cheerfully, "Yes, I'm fine and thanks for coming."

As one sunny day followed another she almost forgot how much the rat had frightened her. "It's dead or gone away," she assured herself.

When she saw it again she stood and stared disbelieving. It crossed the shed in the same unhurried way and she watched, not able to move. A huge rat, there was no doubt about it.

This time Miss Verney didn't rush to Tom's cottage to be reassured. She managed to get to the kitchen, still holding the empty yellow pail, slammed the door and locked it. Then she shut and bolted all the windows. This done, she took off her shoes, lay down, pulled the blankets over her head and listened to her hammering heart.

> *I'm the monarch of all I survey.*
> *My right, there is none to dispute.*

That was the way the rat walked.

In the close darkness she must have dozed, for suddenly she was sitting at a desk in the sun copying proverbs into a ruled book: "Evil Communications corrupt good manners. Look before you leap. Patience is a virtue, good temper a blessing," all the way up to Z. Z would be something to do with zeal or zealous. But how did they manage about X? What about X?

Thinking this, she slept, then woke, put on the light, took two tuinal tablets and slept again, heavily. When she next opened her eyes it was morning, the unwound bedside clock had stopped, but she guessed the time from the light and hurried into the kitchen waiting for Tom's car to pass. The room was stuffy and airless but she didn't dream of opening the window. When she saw the car approaching she ran out into the road and waved it down. It was as if fear had given her wings and once more she moved lightly and quickly.

"Tom, Tom."

He stopped.

"Oh, Tom, the rat's still there. I saw it last evening."

He got down stiffly. Not a young man, but surely surely, a kind man? "I put down enough stuff to kill a dozen rats," he said. "Let's 'ave a look."

He walked across to the shed. She followed, several yards behind, and watched him rattling the old lawnmower, kicking the sacks, trampling the hay and nettles.

"No rat 'ere," he said at last.

"Well there was one," she said.

"Not 'ere."

"It was a huge rat," she said.

Tom had round brown eyes, honest eyes, she'd thought. But now they were sly, mocking, even hostile.

"Are you sure it wasn't a pink rat?" he said.

She knew that the bottles in her dustbin were counted and discussed in the village. But Tom, who she liked so much?

"No," she managed to say steadily. "An ordinary color but very large. Don't they say that some rats now don't care about poison? Super rats."

Tom laughed. "Nothing of that sort round 'ere."

She said: "I asked Mr. Slade, who cuts the grass, to clear out the shed and he said he would but I think he's forgotten."

"Mr. Slade is a very busy man," said Tom. "He can't clear out the shed just when you tell him. You've got to wait. Do you expect him to leave his work and waste his time looking for what's not there?"

"No," she said, "of course not. But I think it ought to be done." (She stopped herself from saying: "I can't because I'm afraid.")

"Now you go and make yourself a nice cup of tea," Tom said, speaking in a more friendly voice. "There's no rat in your shed." And he went back to his car.

Miss Verney slumped heavily into the kitchen armchair. "He doesn't believe me. I can't stay alone in this place, not with that monster a few yards away. I can't do it." But another cold voice persisted: "Where will you go? With what money? Are you really such a coward as all that?"

After a time Miss Verney got up. She dragged what furniture there was away from the walls so that she would know that nothing lurked in the corners and decided to keep the windows looking onto the shed shut and bolted. The others she opened but only at the top. Then she made a large parcel of all the food that the rat could possibly smell—cheese, bacon, ham, cold meat, practically everything ... she'd give it to Mrs. Randolph, the cleaning woman, later.

"But no more confidences." Mrs. Randolph would be as sceptical as Tom had been. A nice woman but a gossip, she wouldn't be able to resist telling her cronies about the giant, almost certainly imaginary, rat terrorizing her employer.

Next morning Mrs. Randolph said that a stray dog had upset the large dustbin. She'd had to pick everything up from the floor of the shed. "It wasn't a dog" thought Miss Verney, but she only suggested that two stones on the lid turned the other way up would keep the dog off.

When she saw the size of the stones she nearly said aloud: "I defy any rat to get that lid off."

Miss Verney had always been a careless, not a fussy, woman. Now all that changed. She spent hours every day sweeping, dusting, arranging the cupboards and putting fresh paper into the drawers. She pounced on every speck of dust with a dustpan. She tried to convince herself that as long as she kept her house spotlessly clean the rat would keep to the shed, not to wonder what she would do if, after all, she encountered it.

"I'd collapse," she thought, "that's what I'd do."

After this she'd start with fresh energy, again fearfully sweeping under the bed, behind cupboards. Then feeling too tired to eat, she would beat up an egg in cold milk, add a good deal of whisky and sip it slowly. "I don't need a lot of food now." But her work in the house grew slower and slower, her daily walks shorter and shorter. Finally the walks stopped. "Why should I bother?" As she never answered letters, letters ceased to arrive, and when Tom knocked at the door one day to ask how she was: "Oh I'm quite all right," she said and smiled.

He seemed ill at ease and didn't speak about rats or clearing the shed out. Nor did she.

"Not seen you about lately," he said.

"Oh I go the other way now."

When she shut the door after him she thought: "And I imagined I liked him. How very strange."

"No pain?" the doctor asked.

"It's just an odd feeling," said Miss Verney.

The doctor said nothing. He waited.

"It's as if all my blood was running backwards. It's rather horrible really. And then for a while sometimes I can't move. I mean if I'm holding a cup I have to drop it because there's no life in my arm."

"And how long does this last?"

"Not long. Only a few minutes I suppose. It just seems a long time."

"Does it happen often?"

"Twice lately."

The doctor thought he'd better examine her. Eventually he left the room and came back with a bottle half full of pills. "Take these three times a day—don't forget, it's important. Long before they're finished I'll come and see you. I'm going to give you some injections that may help, but I'll have to send away for those."

As Miss Verney was gathering her things together before leaving the surgery he asked in a casual voice: "Are you on the telephone?"

"No," said Miss Verney, "but I have an arrangement with some people."

"You told me. But those people are some way off, aren't they?"

"I'll get a telephone," said Miss Verney making up her mind. "I'll see about it at once."

"Good. You won't be so lonely."

"I suppose not."

"Don't go moving the furniture about, will you? Don't lift heavy weights. Don't . . ." ("Oh Lord," she thought, "is he going to say 'Don't drink!'—because that's impossible!") . . . "Don't worry," he said.

When Miss Verney left his surgery she felt relieved but tired and she walked very slowly home. It was quite a long walk for she lived in the less prosperous part of the village, near the row of council houses. She had never minded that. She was protected by tall thick hedges and a tree or two. Of course it had taken her some time to get used to the children's loud shrieking and the women who stood outside their doors to gossip. At first they stared at her with curiosity and some disapproval, she couldn't help feeling, but they'd soon found out that she was harmless.

The child Deena, however, was a very different matter.

Most of the village boys were called Jack, Willie, Stan and so on—the girls' first names were more elaborate. Deena's mother had gone one better than anyone else and christened her daughter Undine.

Deena—as everyone called her—was a tall plump girl of about twelve with a pretty, healthy but rather bovine face. She never joined the shrieking games, she never played football with dustbin lids. She apparently spent all her spare time standing at the gate of her mother's house silently, unsmilingly, staring at everyone who passed.

Miss Verney had long ago given up trying to be friendly. So much did the child's cynical eyes depress her that she would cross over the road to avoid her, and sometimes was guilty of the cowardice of making sure Deena wasn't there before setting out.

Now she looked anxiously along the street and was relieved that it was empty. "Of course," she told herself, "it's getting cold. When winter comes they'll all stay indoors."

Not that Deena seemed to mind cold. Only a few days ago, looking out of the window, Miss Verney had seen her standing outside—oblivious of the bitter wind—staring at the front door as though, if she looked hard enough, she could see through the wood and find out what went on in the silent house—what Miss Verney did with herself all day.

One morning soon after her visit to the doctor Miss Verney woke feeling very well and very happy. Also she was not at all certain where she was. She lay luxuriating in the feeling of renewed youth, renewed health, and slowly recognized the various pieces of furniture.

"Of course," she thought when she drew the curtains. "What a funny place to end up in."

The sky was pale blue. There was no wind. Watching the still trees she sang softly to herself: "The day of days." She had always sung "The day of days" on her birthday. Poised between two years—last year, next year—she never felt any age at all. Birthdays were a pause, a rest.

In the midst of slow dressing she remembered the rat for the first time. But that seemed something that had happened long ago. "Thank God I didn't tell anybody else how frightened I was. As soon as they give me a telephone I'll ask Letty Baker to tea. She'll know exactly the sensible thing to do."

Out of habit she ate, swept and dusted but even more slowly than usual and with long pauses, when leaning on the handle of her tall, old-fashioned, carpet sweeper she stared out at the trees. "Goodbye, summer. Goodbye goodbye," she hummed. But in spite of sad songs she never lost the certainty of health, of youth.

All at once she noticed, to her surprise, that it was getting dark. "And I haven't emptied the dustbin."

She got to the shed carrying the small yellow plastic pail and saw that the big dustbin wasn't there. For once Mrs. Randolph must have slipped up and left it outside the gate. Indeed it was so.

She first brought in the lid, easy, then turned the heavy bin onto its side and kicked it along. But this was slow. Growing impatient, she picked it up, carried it into the shed and looked for the stones that had defeated the dog, the rat. They too were missing and she realized that Mrs. Randolph, a hefty young woman in a hurry, must have taken out the bin, stones and all. They would be in the road where the dustmen had thrown them. She went to look and there they were.

She picked up the first stone and, astonished at its weight, immediately dropped it. But lifted it again and staggered to the shed, then leaned breathless against the cold wall. After a few minutes she breathed more easily, was less exhausted, and the determination to prove to herself that she was quite well again drove her into the road to pick up the second stone.

After a few steps she felt that she had been walking for a long time, for years, weighed down by an impossible weight, and now her strength was gone and she couldn't any more. Still, she reached the shed, dropped the stone and said: "That's all now, that's the lot. Only the yellow plastic pail to tackle." She'd fix the stones tomorrow. The yellow pail was light, full of paper, eggshells, stale bread. Mrs. Verney lifted it. . . .

She was sitting on the ground with her back against the dustbin and her legs stretched out, surrounded by torn paper and eggshells. Her skirt had ridden up and there was a slice of stale bread on her bare knee. She felt very cold and it was nearly dark.

"What happened," she thought, "did I faint or something? I must go back to the house."

She tried to get up but it was as if she were glued to the ground. "Wait," she thought. "Don't panic. Breathe deeply. Relax." But when she tried again she was lead. "This has happened before. I'll be all right soon," she told herself. But darkness was coming on very quickly.

Some women passed on the road and she called to them. At first: "Could you please . . . I'm so sorry to trouble you . . ." but the wind had got up and was blowing against her and no one heard. "Help!" she called. Still no one heard.

Tightly buttoned up, carrying string bags, heads in headscarves, they passed and the road was empty.

With her back against the dustbin, shivering with cold, she prayed: "God, don't leave me here. Dear God, let someone come. Let someone come!"

When she opened her eyes she was not at all surprised to see a figure leaning on her gate.

"Deena! Deena!" she called, trying to keep the hysterical relief out of her voice.

Deena advanced cautiously, stood a few yards off and contemplated Miss Verney lying near the dustbin with an expressionless face.

"Listen Deena," said Miss Verney. "I'm afraid I'm not very well. Will you please ask your mother—your mum—to telephone to the doctor. He'll come I think. And if only she could help me back into the house. I'm very cold. . . ."

Deena said: "It's no good my asking mum. She doesn't like you and she doesn't want to have anything to do with you. She hates stuck up people. Everybody knows that you shut yourself up to get drunk. People can hear you falling about. 'She ought to take more water with it,' my mum says. Sleep it off, lady,'' said this horrible child, skipping away.

Miss Verney didn't try to call her back or argue. She knew that it was useless. A numb weak feeling slowly took possession of her. Stronger than cold. Stronger than fear. It was a great unwillingness to do anything more at all—it was almost resignation. Even if someone else came, would she call again for help. Could she? Fighting the cold numbness she made a last tremendous effort to move, at any rate to jerk the bread off her knee, for now her fear of the rat, forgotten all day, began to torment her.

It was impossible.

She strained her eyes to see into the corner where it would certainly appear—the corner with the old chair and carpet, the corner with the bundle of hay. Would it attack at once or would it wait until it was sure that she couldn't move? Sooner or later it would come. So Miss Verney waited in the darkness for the Super Rat.

It was the postman who found her. He had a parcel of books for her and he left them as usual in the passage. But he couldn't help noticing that all the lights were on and all the doors open. Miss Verney was certainly not in the cottage.

"I suppose she's gone out. But so early and such a cold morning?"

Uneasy, he looked back at the gate and saw the bundle of clothes near the shed.

He managed to lift her and got her into the kitchen armchair. There was an open bottle of whisky on the table and he tried to force her to drink some, but her teeth were tightly clenched and the whisky spilled all over her face.

He remembered that there was a telephone in the house where he was to deliver next. He must hurry.

In less time than you'd think, considering it was a remote village, the doctor appeared and shortly afterwards the ambulance.

Miss Verney died that evening in the nearest hospital without

recovering consciousness. 'The doctor said she died of shock and cold. He was treating her for a heart condition, he said.
  "Very widespread now—a heart condition."

Born in the West Indies of a Creole mother and a Welsh father, the still beautiful Jean Rhys lived a Bohemian life in Paris after her marriage. She began to write when her marriage broke up. Her early stories were published in the 1920's. About 1940 Ms. Rhys retired to the country but was rediscovered in the 1950's living quietly and writing in Devon.

"Your hair has grown in again.
Nobody will see a thing."

The Windward Islands

BY ALFRED ANDERSCH

A native, a tourist . . . and trauma.

IT was much too early. As they left the Deutsches Museum the day
before, Sir Thomas Wilkins had asked Franz Kien to come to the
Hotel Vier Jahreszeiten at two o'clock but it was only one when he
got out of the streetcar at Odeonsplatz. He had one mark seventy
in his pocket and decided to have a cup of coffee at the Café
Rottenhöfer. Late that afternoon, the Englishman would pay him
for his services as a guide: two tours; he was hoping for twenty or
thirty marks.

Instead of turning directly into Residenzstrasse where the café
was situated, he detoured by way of Theatinerstrasse and Vis-
cardistrasse, so as to avoid passing the National Socialist Memorial
and having to raise his arm in the Hitler salute.

At that time of day the café was almost empty. A few women. At
one table two SA men were sitting. Franz Kien had not expected
to meet anyone he knew. As recently as the previous fall the Café

Rottenhöfer had been the meeting place of "his" group in the Young Communist League. Franz Lehner, Ludwig Kessel, Gebhard Homolka and a few others, plus the girls: Adelheid Sennhauser, Sophia Weber, and Else Laub. Franz, Ludwig, Gebhard, and the others were still in Dachau; Adelheid was in some women's prison. Franz Kien had once tried to look up Else Laub, but her mother had opened the door by a crack and said in an angry whisper: "What do you want? Go away! We're under police surveillance!"—in a tone suggesting that Franz Kien was to blame for the attitude of the Gestapo. Suddenly he caught sight of Wolfgang Fischer. He was sitting at a table in the rear of the café, talking with young men unknown to Franz Kein.

Franz Kien was delighted. He went directly to Fischer's table and held out his hand.

"Wolfgang!" he said. "It's great to see you!"

Wolfgang Fischer had not been a Communist but a member of the International Socialist Combat League. Quite as a matter of course, Franz Kien thought in the past tense, though he knew that small remnants of certain Communist and Socialist groups still existed illegally. The Young Communists had regarded the ISCL as an eccentric sect; its members were vegetarians, teetotallers, and believers in moral purity. They were not Marxists but supporters of a Heidelberg philosopher by the name of Leonard Nelson. Though they obviously felt themselves to be an elite, they were modest and reserved, and for that they were well liked. They had been in close contact with the Young Communists, gone on excursions with them, and attended their meetings with a view to discussion.

Wolfgang Fischer raised his head and looked at Franz Kien, but did not take his hand.

"Yes," he said. "Isn't it great to see a Jew?"

Wolfgang Fischer was a few years older than Franz Kien. He was studying chemistry at Munich University. He was stockily built, with short-cropped red hair and the reddish, freckly skin that goes with it. Everything about him was hard: the small blue eyes with their red brows, the tight skin over his muscles and bones. As a long-distance runner he had been prominent in workers' sports activities; Franz Kien had once watched him running the ten thousand meters; he ran like a machine, quickening his pace only in the last five hundred meters, so as to add another lap to his lead over all the others, who were already one or more laps behind. At the finish he had shown no signs of fatigue. He was a Socialist from ethical conviction. In conversations with Franz Kien he had taken the view that socialism would win out, not as a consequence of necessary dialectical processes, but because it was grounded in justice. Modestly, calmly, and matter-of-factly, he expounded the doctrines of Kant and Leonard Nelson. The eighteen-year-old Franz Kien, a beginner in Marxism, could not stand up to him in discussion; he had merely felt that if Wolfgang Fischer was right the decision in favor of socialism was a matter of pure will, and instinctively he doubted the efficacy of pure will. But he felt drawn to Wolfgang Fischer, to this resolute man who spoke gently to him and treated him with patient friendliness.

Such a sentence from Fischer's mouth came as a complete surprise. Franz Kien was so taken aback that he could think of no reply. Slowly he withdrew his hand, conscious that he was blushing with embarrassment.

"What do you mean by that?" he asked finally.

He had been meaning, quite as a matter of course, to take the empty chair at the table.

"What I mean?" Franz Kien had never heard Fischer speak in such a tone. "Don't play innocent! You know perfectly well. I mean that today all you Germans feel the same way about us Jews."

He averted his eyes from Kien and spoke into the air. For some reason that he himself did not understand until later, Franz Kien was unable to tell Wolfgang Fischer that he had spent the spring in a concentration camp and that he still had to report to the Gestapo once a week.

Maybe I could tell him if I were sitting at the table with him, he thought. But as it was, standing, aware of his flushed face, he only managed to say:

"You must be off your rocker!"

"It's easy to say that to a Jew today," Wolfgang Fischer replied instantly. He motioned with his shoulders to the young man sitting beside him, who was looking uncomfortable, obviously embarrassed by the scene. "Please go away. We're leaving for Palestine in a few days and we have a lot of things to discuss."

Franz Kien turned abruptly and left the café. In his confusion he failed to notice which way he was going, but just on time he saw the SS men standing motionless beside the memorial tablet and changed his direction. On his way down Residenzstrasse toward Franz-Josef-Platz, he remembered that he had wanted a cup of coffee. But then Fischer had expelled him from the Café Rottenhöfer. Little by little, it occurred to him how he might have answered Fischer. For instance, he could have said: "The ISCL people have not been arrested. There are no ISCL members in Dachau. Not even Jewish members. In Dachau there were only Communists, Communists, Communists." Then he remembered the middle-class Jews from Nuremberg, whom he had seen in Dachau.

He went to another café where he had never been. It was across the way from the Hoftheater and consisted of one tiny room. He would have liked a piece of almond cake with his coffee, but he hadn't enough money. In those days he didn't smoke. After a while he succeeded in shrugging off the incident with Wolfgang Fischer. It was mad, simply mad! After his coffee, because the cake had been denied him, he felt a faint but gnawing pang of hunger, for which there was no real justification because he had eaten an adequate lunch at home. He knew he would carry his hunger pang around with him all afternoon, while showing Sir Thomas Wilkins the town. He would keep hoping that Wilkins would interrupt the tour and treat him to tea and cake. At the bakery next to the Franziskaner he bought two rolls and ate them, standing at a doorway. That stilled his hunger.

"An Englishman with the title 'Sir,' " his brother had lectured him, "is always addressed by the title and his first name." Consequently Franz Kien had avoided the direct form of address while guiding Sir Thomas Wilkins through the Deutsches Museum. The day before yesterday, Sir Thomas Wilkins had bought a Wagner score from Franz Kien's elder brother and asked him on the occasion whether he knew a student or other cultivated young man who might show him around Munich. Franz Kien's brother worked in a music store on Maximilianstrasse. Franz Kien himself was unemployed. He had been unemployed for three years.

"I haven't the faintest idea how to show anyone around Munich," he had objected. "Besides, I don't speak English."

"The gentleman speaks German," his brother had replied. "And you know Munich very well. Pull yourself together. Sir Thomas is a high English colonial official. It's not every day that you meet such a man. Besides, it's a job." The lesson about the form of address had followed. Franz Kien could see that his brother would have liked to guide the Englishman himself.

"I just don't feel like it," he said.

"I've already accepted for you," said his brother. "Eleven tomorrow morning at the Vier Jahreszeiten." He inspected his brother. "Your hair has grown in again. Nobody will see a thing."

Franz Kien's hair had been shaved off in Dachau, and had taken an amazing length of time, nearly all summer, to grow in.

All evening he had racked his brains about how to show someone around Munich, but no ideas had come to him; he had felt paralyzed.

After meeting Wilkins in the hotel lobby, he had awkwardly suggested a number of possible itineraries. Suddenly Wilkins had raised his head, looked out through the plate-glass window into the rain, and announced that he would like to visit the Deutsches Museum. It turned out that he had already been in Munich several times, though not in the last twenty years. He spoke so knowledgeably of Munich that Franz Kien couldn't help wondering why he needed a guide. Of course there wasn't much else one could do in the rain, but Franz Kien nevertheless had the impression that the Englishman had wanted to help him out of his perplexity. With a sense of relief, Franz Kien stood up to go, for surely no guide was required for a visit to a museum, but without a moment's hesitation the old gentleman said amiably that of course they would go together. He ordered a cab. It was a long time since Franz Kien had ridden in a taxi.

He was glad that Wilkins expressed no desire to see the mines.

The mines in the Deutsches Museum were a bore. Wilkins explained an 1813 model of a Watt beam engine with water pump, the Bessemer process of converting iron into steel, and other inventions of which Franz Kien hadn't the faintest glimmer. Despite his English accent he spoke excellent German. He said he had studied in Dresden in 1888. In the fall of 1933, the year 1888 had a legendary ring in Franz Kien's ears.

At two o'clock Wilkins suggested lunch. He wanted, he said, to "eat something typical of Munich in a typical Munich restaurant, perhaps *Leberkäs* or *Schweinswürstl*"—two of the dishes he remembered. Franz Kien pondered. It was hard to find anything in the vicinity of the museum. Then he remembered a restaurant on Paulanerplatz, where he and his Party friends had often met. Under the Englishman's large black umbrella they crossed the bridge over the green-foaming Isar and made their way through the streets of the Au district. The proprietor recognized Franz and said: "Hm, so here you are again."—but no more. Possibly he was as displeased as Else Laub's mother to see Franz Kien again, but he didn't show it, he merely dropped the subject, and naturally Franz Kien was just as glad that he should ask no questions in the Englishman's presence.

There was neither *Leberkäse* nor *Schweinswürstl*, but there was fresh *Milzwurst*, so they sat at the freshly scrubbed table eating fried *Milzwurst* with potato salad and drinking beer. Over the meal Sir Thomas Wilkins told Franz Kien that his last post had been that of civil governor of Malta; before that he had been military governor of the Windward Islands, and before that a judge in East Africa. It seemed to be of the utmost importance to him that Franz Kien should understand the difference between a civil governor and a military governor. He had the most to say of the Windward Islands. "My home was in St. George's, Grenada," he said. "I went from island to island on my yacht. But there was very little to do. Those people don't quarrel much." He fell silent and seemed to be dreaming. "But it's very hot down there," he said then. "My sister was always knitting. When her ball of wool fell to the floor and I stooped to pick it up, I was bathed in sweat."

Franz Kien found this mention of Wilkins' sister so unusual that he ventured to ask if he were married.

"Why, of course," Wilkins replied with alacrity. "I have two children. They're grown up now. My wife lives in London. We see each other now and then. My sister has been keeping house for me in the last few years."

And quite naturally, without irony, he went on: "A man should definitely have been married once. But it needn't be for his lifetime."

They went back to the museum. Wilkins was enthusiastic about the planetariums. He kept going back and forth between the Ptolemaic and the Copernican planetarium, explaining the differences to Franz Kien. Together they climbed into the car under the mobile model, from which one could follow the earth in its orbit. Up until then these planetariums had never meant much to Franz Kien. Despite the light effects in the darkness, he had found them dull and boring. And besides, he had never taken much interest in the stars and constellations. He had been unemployed since the age of sixteen and politics had been his sole preoccupation. (In Dachau the prisoners had been forbidden to leave the barracks after dark.)

That night he had taken out his atlas and located the Windward Islands. They formed the southernmost archipelago of the Lesser Antilles.

Today he had resolved to greet Wilkins with a "Good day, Sir Thomas," but when the Englishman entered the lobby, the words refused to come out and he had only bowed. Wilkins had simply addressed him as Franz; it hadn't sounded condescending.

"What will you show me today, Franz?" he now asked.

"As if I showed you anything yesterday!" said Franz Kien. "You showed me the Deutsches Museum."

Wilkins smiled. "Today the weather is perfect," he said. "Now it's your turn."

The weather was indeed perfect, a fine September afternoon. Franz Kien led Wilkins through narrow, almost deserted streets which began directly behind the hotel, to the church of Sankt Anna in Lehel. He did not know whether Wilkins was interested in churches or art, but he had decided to show the foreigner a few of the things that he, Franz Kien, loved in his home town. In the church he spoke like a real guide about Johann Michael Fischer and the Asam brothers. He couldn't tell what impression this piece of Bavarian baroque was making on the Englishman. On a man who bought Wagner scores! In the oval interior Sir Thomas Wilkins sat down in one of the pews, but instead of studying the Asam frescoes merely looked into space. Franz Kien stood beside him and waited. The pew was so narrow that the Englishman had to raise his knees. He had a gray mustache. Even now, in his somewhat absent state, his eyes had a friendly look. Up ahead of them a woman was kneeling.

On Galeriestrasse a blue streetcar was ringing its bell. They went to the Hofgarten. At that time the lime trees had not yet been cut down and the concert pavilion was a weatherbeaten yellow under the early-autumn foliage. They walked under the arcade and Franz Kien stopped in front of the Rottmann frescoes. The Greek landscapes faded into surfaces of twilight blue, brown and red. It was easy to see that these frescoes would not last much longer. Wilkins said that Greece was just like that. He spoke of the trips to the Greek islands that he had taken from Malta.

They emerged from the park at Odeonsplatz, which Wilkins remembered well. For the first time they saw SA men in their brown uniforms. There had been a few in the Deutsches Museum. Franz Kien had expected Wilkins to remark on them, perhaps even to ask questions about the political situation in Germany, but he had said nothing. Instead, he asked Franz Kien how long he had been unemployed.

"We've been having a bad economic crisis in England too," he said after Franz Kien had replied. "But things are looking up now. They will here too. You're sure to find work soon."

He seemed to be looking at the brown and black uniforms as he looked at everything, calmly and matter-of-factly. Franz Kien kept wondering whether to tell him about his stay in Dachau, but he couldn't make up his mind to do so.

He managed to steer Sir Thomas past the Feldherrenhalle into Theatinerstrasse without his catching sight of the National Socialist memorial. When they came to Perusastrasse, he stopped and said: "If we go straight ahead, we'll come to the Rathaus. It's hideous. If we turn right, we'll come to the Frauenkirche." After a moment's hesitation he added: "To tell the truth, it's hideous too. Would you like to see it?"

Wilkins laughed. "No, of course not, if it's hideous. Show me something nice."

Franz Kien led him into Peruastrasse past the Main Post Office to the Alter Hof. He hadn't been there for a long time and remembered it as being more interesting, more mysterious than it actually was. In reality, the Alter Hof was merely a rectangular group of old, relatively well-built houses occupied by government offices. Still, there was the oriel with the "Golden Roof." Standing there with Wilkins, Franz Kien felt ill at ease. Maybe he had made a mistake in coming here, though Wilkins admired the Alter Hof and said it reminded him of certain medieval buildings in Edinburgh.

Possibly because of this feeling of uncertainty, he now, instead of leading Wilkins past the Food Market to the old Rathaus, headed for Franz-Josef-Platz, which was nearer. There, to Franz Kien's dismay, the Englishman took an interest in the Residenz, first examining the south façade, then despite Franz Kien's attempts to guide him in a different direction, walking around the western wing.

Across from the Café Rottenhöfer, Franz Kien stopped, he pointed out the building across the street and said: "That's the Preysing Palace. It's the finest rococo palace in Munich. Down there, on the wall of the Feldherrenhalle, the National Socialists have put up a memorial tablet. Where the two SS men are standing."

Looking down Residenzstrasse, Wilkins saw the two motionless figures. Even their steel helmets were black.

"Memorial tablet?" he said. "What is it in memory of?"

"The Hitler putsch of 1923," said Franz Kien. "The first attempt of the National Socialists to take power. They staged a demonstration and the police fired. A few people were killed."

"I remember," said Wilkins. "Didn't General Ludendorff take part?"

"Yes." Franz Kien didn't know whether there was irony in his voice when he said: "He was the only one who didn't lie down when the police fired."

"The police must have had instructions not to hit him," said Wilkins. He added: "But I don't mean to imply that General Ludendorff wasn't a brave man."

Franz Kien looked across at the Café Rottenhöfer. Wolfgang Fischer must have left long ago. Franz Kien could have told Sir Thomas about the night of the Hitler putsch. In the middle of the night his father, who worshiped General Ludendorff, had put on his infantry captain's uniform and gone out to take part in the putsch. How gray and lifeless the apartment—situated in a middle-class suburb—had seemed when he was gone! Franz Kien had been nine at the time. That night he had hoped his father would return victorious and fill the night-blind wardrobe mirror in the the uniform without a word. He had died a few years later, but not too soon to see Franz join the Young Communists. Franz thought of his dead father. What would he have said about Dachau? Franz Kien sometimes basked in the illusion that his father would have disapproved of Dachau, especially if he, his son, had told him what went on there. But his father had been a Jew hater, an Anti-Semite like Ludendorff. And now Wolfgang Fischer was emigrating to Palestine.

"Everybody seems to be saluting the tablet," said Wilkins.

"It's compulsory," said Franz Kien. "But we don't have to pass it," he added, taking it for granted that the Englishman would have no desire to pass the memorial. And pointing to Viscardigasse, "We can take that street over there to Odeonsplatz. Everybody who doesn't want to salute goes that way. It's not much longer."

He tried to smile when he explained: "Everybody in Munich calls it Goldbrick Street."

"Goldbrick Street?" Wilkins repeated. "Ah, I see."

After a moment's thought he said: "No, I'd rather go straight ahead."

That, Franz Kien realized later on, after giving a good deal of thought to his stroll with Sir Thomas Wilkins, was when he should have spoken up. He need only have said: "Excuse me if I leave

you for just a few moments. I'll meet you on Odeonsplatz."
Perhaps, no certainly, Wilkins would have understood and either
said nothing or asked him to explain. True, Franz Kien had no
idea how Sir Thomas would have reacted to his explanation.
Quite possibly he had no objection to the National Socialist
regime. He might even have sympathized with the Nazis. It was
certain that he felt no affection for the Communists.

But Franz Kien had lacked presence of mind. Once he had
failed to speak up, there was nothing he could do but go on at
Wilkin's side. Instead of escaping while there was still time, he had
engaged in futile speculation: what would happen when Sir
Thomas passed the memorial without saluting? Franz Kien knew
that two Gestapo plainclothesmen standing across the street from
the memorial, in the doorway of the Residenz, would come up to
Wilkins and demand an explanation, but would withdraw with
apologies when he—as haughtily as possible, Franz Kien
hoped—produced his English passport. The speculation was futile
because, while Franz Kien was still visualizing this easy little vic-
tory, he saw the Englishman raise his right arm in the Hitler salute.
Quite mechanically, he followed suit, not looking at the memorial
across the street, but observing Wilkin's face, which was in between. He saw that it took on the same expressionless look as
when, picking up his knees in the narrow church pew, Wilkins had
sat staring into space.

They lowered their arms at the same time. Wilkins suggested tea
at the Annast. They found a table by the window with a view of
the Theatinerkirche and the end of Briennerstrasse.

While Franz Kien was still wondering whether the Englishman
might not have given the Hitler salute because he thought it un-
worthy of a gentleman to take Goldbrick Street, he heard him
saying: "In a foreign country I like to do what the inhabitants do.
One understands them better if one adopts their customs."

"I've heard," said Franz Kien, "that an Englishman is always an
Englishman, regardless of where he goes."

"Oh yes, we're always Englishmen," said Wilkins. "But we try
to understand."

Franz Kien looked at the one time civil governor of Malta, military governor of the Windward Islands, and judge in East Africa. An Englishman who, with expressionless features, studied the ways of the natives. The natives of Malta and the Windward Islands, of East Africa and Munich. This Englishman, in all likelihood, had lost all desire to rule. He was content to sail from island to island on his governor's yacht and settle disputes when asked to do so. A dispute that could not be settled was probably inconceivable to him, Franz Kien thought. It would have been useless to tell him about Dachau.

No, Franz Kien thought, when it was too late, it would not have been useless. On the strength of what he had told him, Sir Thomas Wilkins would probably have submitted a confidential report to his government.

Wilkins handed him a folded hundred-mark note.

"That's too much," said Franz Kien.

"It's very little," Wilkins replied, taking the same tone as when he had decreed that Franz Kien should accompany him to the Deutsches Museum. He gave Franz Kien his card. On it there was only his name, and, in the lower right-hand corner: St. James's Club, London S.W. 1.

"I travel a good deal," he said. "If you should like to write to me, Franz, a letter will always reach me at this address."

Franz Kien never wrote to him. After the war, on his first visit to London, he went to the St. James's Club. The man at the reception desk looked through the register. Then he said: "I'm sorry, sir. Sir Thomas Wilkins died on March 5, 1941."

Franz Kien was sorry too. As he stepped out into St. James's Square, he could see Sir Thomas—as he now called him in his thoughts—skirting the grass plot at the center of the square, turning into Pall Mall, and receding from view. That day in Munich he had receded from view on Promenadeplatz in exactly the same way, a tall old gentleman wearing a light raincoat and carrying a tightly rolled black umbrella. Franz had taken the streetcar home. On arriving, he had again consulted the atlas and tried to imagine the wind which was so strong that in spite of the heat the islands that lay in its path had taken their name from it.

Alfred Andersch is one of Europe's leading writers of short stories and novels. In his youth, he was a political prisoner in Dachau for six months. Later he became a newspaper editor. He fought as a German soldier in World War II and was a prisoner of war in the U.S. Ralph Manheim is his distinguished translator.

"He was making a bee-line for the cliff,
and as he neared it without changing the pace
I began to feel uneasy . . ."

The Man on the Gray Horse

BY E.G. CHIPULINA

Engaging right through the final revelation.

HE stood facing me across the horseshoe bar with sightless intro-
spective gaze, and perhaps not quite sober. He looked haggard
and strangely smaller; his hair had become sparse and gray, his
moustache heavier. Time's subtle touch had dulled his virile look,
yet the likeness was there—that rare blend of Latin and Teutonic
features amicably come to terms. Blurred memories began to
focus in my mind, and suddenly a name came hurtling at me out
of the past.

I had been a mere boy then, he a grown man, and our contact
brief. My chances of being recognized in return were slim, and—
lest it led to some embarrassing misunderstanding—I gave up
trying to catch his eye. But in the end a powerful curiosity got the
better of my native discretion, and I decided to risk a snub. As he
persisted in remaining unaware of my approach, I had to clear my
throat several times before attracting a glance from him—the kind

of sidelong glance usually reserved for importuning touts. Undaunted, however, I went straight to the point.

"I believe I know you. You're Mr Steffan, aren't you?"

He nodded, rather like a bored celebrity used to being recognized in public.

I persisted, my voice full of apology. "I don't suppose my name would mean anything to you. Hornsby—Jerry Hornsby."

I imagine it was my earnestness more than the name itself that caught his grudging attention. "Hornsby?"

"Yes. Perhaps you recall we stayed for a time at Villa . . . this was quite a few years ago; the name eludes me—I mean the Monteiros' home in Madeira. . . ."

"Quinta Miranda?"

"Well . . . possibly. I was only a child then. You may remember my mother—or, better still, her cousin Amecia who used to stay there often."

"Amecia! Of course." He raised his glass absently, peered through it, and gulped down half its contents. Then, for the first time, he examined me with some curiosity. "So you are. . . ." He snapped his fingers clumsily. "What was the name again?"

"Jerry."

The effort of thinking back showed in his perplexed look. He kept stroking his chin as if this stimulated his memory. "My God!" he said. "How long ago was that?"

How long ago? It was not so much a question as a cry of bewilderment—perhaps at the brevity of life.

The nineteen-thirties! It may have been a fool's paradise that we lived in, but I still recall those twilight years with unashamed nostalgia. Mine was a very ordinary middle-class family, quite deaf to the rumblings that foreboded war and social upheaval—our rural air was a bad conductor of unpleasant sounds. The memory of that quiet, unhurried life remains my private refuge from contemporary noise and bustle. I have no quarrel with progress, no secret ambition to gag the hairy ones and dump their amplifiers in the river, or set the clock of aeronautics back to the balloon age. If the louder products and by-products of technology happen to disagree with me, the fault is entirely mine—whatever it is that one is supposed to be with, I simply am not. The truth is that I was brought up in a dull environment, where a train ride out of town or the advent of a traveling circus was a major event. I abused a fertile imagination to provide the missing color, and now that the imagination has become sterile, reality overwhelms me.

Those memories that bring nostalgia are, after all, nothing but revived fancies; but there is an interlude of reality. On the horizon of my tame little world there suddenly loomed up one day the prospect of travel and adventure. My mother, at the time recovering from a long, debilitating illness, had been strongly advised to convalesce for two months at a suitable health resort. My father, who came from a long line of thrifty merchants, could well afford the expense of accompanying her, but not the time away from his business, and though she was normally easy-going and amenable, this time there was no getting round her—she would not hear of staying on her own at a foreign hotel. And there matters seemed to stand.

Then, from an unexpected quarter, came an inspired solution to the problem. On my mother's side we had a Portuguese relative—"Aunt" Amecia I called her, with more politeness than accuracy—who had spent a holiday with us a few years before and corresponded regularly with my mother, who liked her. Women being what they are, she soon learnt of the situation. Back came her reply: she usually stayed over Lent at the country home of her brother-in-law on the island of Madeira; why not join her? The place was an ideal resort, and my mother would be most welcome. At least that was the gist of it. The tone of the invitation was far warmer, more elaborate, and difficult to refuse.

Not only did my mother like the idea, she also sweetly bargained with my strict father to let her take me along too. Since, with the Easter holidays coming up, I would lose little schooling, to my immense delight she got away with it. It was my good fortune that mothers tend to be more than usually attached to belated offspring.

The thought of a sea voyage to an island that I mentally catalogued as exotic and mysterious kept me on tenterhooks while arrangements were being made—the horrifying possibility that my father might yet change his mind made the waiting almost unbearable. But finally the day arrived when I had scrambled up the gangway and the ship's siren was booming above with a Biblical finality. A couple of days later, as we steamed up the estuary of the Tagus, with a pink dawn breaking over the chaotic beauty of the hills of old Lisbon, I was already feeling a seasoned traveler.

Here we were joined by Aunt Amecia, a large, expansive woman, whose every movement from place to place caused a slight commotion. She wore permanent mourning for her husband, a former Portuguese consul at a British West Indian island, where she had learnt to speak English but with a disconcerting tendency to stress the wrong syllable.

"My dear Helen—my *dear* little Jerry!" She embraced us jointly, then singly, tucking me under her heavy arm like a mother hen. "But you are not taking care of yourself," she reproached my mother. "How pale you look! We must make you strong again—our mira*culous* climate will give you new life; you must not worry, dear." Then, *sotto voce*: "And we shall pray fervently to . . ." There was a kind of religious snobbery about the intimacy with which blessed names poured from her lips. She was truly a pious woman, and perhaps—since pious has become almost synonymous with hypocritical—I should emphasize that she was so in a kindly, tolerant way. Much as I objected to her multiple, perfumed kisses I could not seriously dislike her.

My mother was full of womanly curiosity about our future host, whom she had never met. His somewhat grandiose name, Captain Jose-Maria Saldanha Monteiro—which Amecia abbreviated to a simple Jose—impressed me as much as the discovery that he was an ex-cavalryman. He was the widower of Amecia's sister, and had a twenty-year-old daughter living with him.

Late one afternoon, a cloud-topped cone peeped over the rim of the ocean, and the rugged mass of an island, faintly menacing, seemed to be born before my eyes. The light was fading when the ship dropped anchor in the bay of Funchal, across which drifted the warm breath of a fertile land. I was to see little of the capital, but its first impact lingers: in the strangely phosphoric afterglow,

two massive limbs branching downwards from a cleft in the towering heights, and across their feet spread the city like a sequined
mantle.

We spent the night at an hotel, and in the early morning, before
I had a chance to prowl, a car had arrived to fetch us. It was a
well-preserved relic driven by an old chauffeur, equally well-preserved, whom Amecia treated with great familiarity. She kept up
an incessant chatter all the way to the estate—local gossip, family
news, criticism and advice, and frequent appeals for divine inter-
vention in the affairs of her brother-in-law. I was too absorbed in
the utter novelty of my surroundings to listen closely. The winding
mountain roads and frequent stops to cool the overheated engine
stretched the journey disproportionately. We climbed inter-
minably in the heady atmosphere of pine woods; past mighty
gorges and escarpments where the land lay raw-red, bare amid
the dense greenery.

The sun was high when, as the road began to wind downwards
for the first time, the old chauffeur pointed out the Monteiro estate
far below. The cultivated land was terraced down the foothills,
ending in a final sweep that reached a cliff above the sea. Somewhere in a thickly wooded section of the plain hid the house. By
lunchtime we had arrived at Quinta Miranda; a solid mellow building, vaguely melancholic, that appeared unexpectedly like some
jungle dwelling in a clearing.

My first impression of Captain Monteiro was colored by the
influence of Hollywood and the more extravagant fiction I was
then addicted to. The arch-villain, whose hard set face filled the
screen every time the hero's happiness seemed assured, or whose
shadow darkened every printed page of melodrama, now stood
before me in the flesh. He had slightly oriental features, with black
eyebrows fossilized in a curve of disdain, and a domed bald head
whose tan betrayed his open-air life. Of middle height, he was,
despite his years, extremely lithe and well-proportioned. He wore
jodhpurs and an open-necked shirt. I looked instinctively for duel-
ing scars on his face but, much to my regret, there were none.

My mother seemed a little overawed by his stiff handshake.
"Madame 'Ornsby. Enchanted!" He spoke precisely, in a rasping

voice. "You are—let me see—Amecia's English cousin? Ver' well; you must make yourself—as you say—perfectly at 'ome." He waved a hand carelessly. "The house and the . . . ah . . . domestics are at your disposal."

At this point his severe gaze fell on me. "So!" His actual remark escapes my memory. Without being a straight question, it demanded some form of acknowledgment, and being incurably shy, I could manage nothing more coherent than an inane little laugh. My mother blushed in sympathy with me, and Aunt Amecia seemed to think the moment opportune to praise me at great length, which manifestly bored the Captain. The arrival of Ines, his daughter, who came in from the garden full of breathless apologies for being late, saved me from further embarrassment.

She was a pale, raven-haired girl with a warmth in her eyes and a simplicity that immediately appealed to me. I did not have to be very observant to notice that her father's presence had a restraining effect on her obvious delight at seeing Amecia. In a while, however, after summoning a white-clad servant to take our luggage upstairs, the Captain briefly excused himself and left the women to their prattle. Ines and my mother seemed to take quite naturally to each other, which I thought was a good thing, for I foresaw the three of them happily engaged in long babbling sessions, with a corresponding reduction of maternal supervision over my own activities.

We settled down smoothly to the routine of the household. It was very leisurely and ideal for my mother. The surroundings were enchanting, the weather not far short of perfect, and there were numerous servants; simple, genial people who would not let her lift a finger to help herself. We rarely saw the Captain, except at mealtimes. He ate sparingly, to which no doubt he owed his fine physique; on the other hand, he drank quite heavily, if without visible effect. He seemed used to Ameica's irrelevant loquacity and generally ignored her except to answer a direct question. For all that, I could sense there was a live-and-let-live relationship between them. Once, presumably for my mother's sake, Monteiro apologized for his lengthy absences:

"The estate is ver' big, you understand? I have much, much

work."

His work, I subsequently gathered (from Amecia's running commentary of events past and present), consisted largely of riding round the estate or shooting, with friends or by himself, up in the wild *serra*. He paid an overseer to look after his property and business. Amecia was shrewd, if repetitivie; candid, if tolerant; she doubted—though she did not put it so crudely—whether her brother-in-law had done a stroke of useful work in his whole life. Even his military career had been brief and undistinguished. Indeed, he soon began to prove disappointing. My villains were villainous on a magnificent scale; this man was merely petty, devoid even of that easy charm which often characterizes the truly idle, the corrupt or the rich. He was courteous in his way, but only with those he considered his social equals. His harsh treatment of the servants profoundly shocked my mother who herself was used to being bullied by our own temperamental cook. It was easy to imagine him lording it over the peasant laborers on his land like a medieval baron over his serfs. Be that as it may, one could not dismiss the man with a shrug. There was about him a certain quality, a kind of animal self-confidence, that could not be ignored—but perhaps I say this with hindsight.

Ines was very friendly. Not surprisingly, she looked forward to the few occasions when they had guests. Sometimes she would corner me after dinner to practice her school English.

"Your mama!" she complained. "She does not correct my mistakes when we talk—she said it is rude to . . . to . . ."

"Interrupt?"

"Yes, yes." Her small exposed small, uneven teeth that somehow enhanced its charm.

Ines must have taken after her mother. The paternal likeness was mirrored in her face, but temperamentally father and daughter seemed poles apart. She had the kind of subdued personality that will lure a shy youngster out of his shell, so that, far from considering it an ordeal, I grew to enjoy chatting with her. Life for the poor girl, though easy, must have been lonely and boring. Moreover, the boredom was aggravated by the need to observe a ridiculous set of rules that smacked of obsessive prudery. She confessed, for instance, to never having bathed in the sea, the wearing of a bathing suit being taboo. Her bedtime had currently been altered from eleven to midnight, but only as a special concession because Amecia was staying. With the capital so inconveniently distant, even the simple amusement of a stroll down a crowded avenue was denied her; to visit the city she had to depend on her father's infrequent trips. In my innocence it baffled me that a grown-up woman should be tied down by the sort of dos and don'ts I had thought everyone left behind at prep. school. I suppose there was more of the feudal overlord in Monteiro than the superficial likeness that had struck me—no doubt he would have approved of the subtle medieval approach to the problem of female virtue. And I suppose, too, he was fortunate in Ines. Had she been a vivacious, restless beauty there would surely have been serious trouble in that household.

Within the first few days, I had begun to slip away on my own, beyond the trim lawns and hibiscus hedges surrounding the house. The Captain had vaguely promised one morning he would get someone called Steffan to take me on a tour of the estate, but in the meantime I was eager to get my own impressions. There was a densely wooded tract of land sloping towards the coast that was begging to be explored. I like solitary places, and here I found that I could roam about for hours without meeting a soul. It was neither wood nor garden, but a wild mixture of both, and quite close to my childish concept of Eden. There was, however, a semblance of order in the confusion, as if someone had originally planned an extension to the house garden and then abandoned the project to nature. Exotic things grew profusely in that warm climate: mangoes and avocado pears, dwarf coconuts and a nameless little fruit that tasted like a cross between a loquat and God knows what—God knows too why I did not go down with acute indigestion.

In the course of my ramblings I discovered a look-out at the summit of the wooded hill. Ornately built of cement inlaid with colored stones and shells, it had an air of neglect, but a magnificent all-round view. Behind were the mountains, and ahead the

Atlantic and the neighboring desert islands, long gray shapes on the horizon like basking sharks. The size of the estate was appreciable from this vantage point. The fringe of the wood stood poised along a ridge, like cavalry about to charge down the slope that ended in an arid plain, and beyond a quilt of sugar cane and sweet potato patches covered the land to the base of the foothills. On the sea side the natural contours were chopped off unsymmetrically by a fifty- or sixty-foot cliff.

The place had a spell that lured me out of bed one morning to catch the sun rising from the ocean. It happened, as the drama was reaching its climax, that a dull rhythmic pounding caught my attention. Someone was riding a horse at full gallop across the plain below, and the sound carried in the still morning air. The horse was gray and seemed very large despite the distance, and and its rider, crouching well forward, was unmistakably the Captain. For some moments I watched with admiration; in this way I had first pictured him, and the reality was not disappointing. The dull gleam of the slanting sun on his bare, bald head, which might well have struck me as ridiculous, seemed somehow to heighten the air of bravado about him. He was making a bee-line for the cliff, and as he neared it without changing the pace I began to feel uneasy, then horrified until, when it seemed inevitable that they would go over, he pulled up sharply no more than a couple of yards from the drop. Before the dust had settled, he began to walk the horse parallel and sickeningly close to the edge. The animal kept twisting this way and that, now backing fitfully, now attempting to prance. It seemed as if it were under some mad compulsion to hurl itself down the precipice. The next moment it became perfectly clear that almost the opposite was true. Monteiro was forcing his mount to conquer its instinctive fear of heights, which apparently he himself did not share. With spur and crop, and imperative commands that reached me, he was thwarting the great beast's frantic attempts to get clear of the danger. I do not know for how long the strange spectacle continued; at last, seeming satisfied, he gave his mount free rein and rode off at an easy canter.

That night I was awakened several times by a suffocating fear as

I fell down a bottomless void. Sometimes I was clinging to an enormous gray horse, sometimes the animal came somersaulting after me. In the morning I was up early again and, driven by a perverse hope that Monteiro would repeat the previous day's performance, I hurried breakfastless to my look-out. The sun was already up, and so was the Captain, in the process of putting his horse through its grim paces.

All the following week I managed to reach my hideout in time to see him arrive punctually with the dawn. At first I was held awestruck, as if witnessing some secret ritual; then, gradually, familiarity began to divest the thing of its mystery. I watched objectively, with the simple admiration I might have felt for a lion tamer on a routine training session. The frightened animal was certainly intent on throwing its rider, but the Captain's horsemanship was superb, his grip ruthless and complete. Common sense warned me he would misjudge one day and go over the edge, with or without his mount. And yet I would as soon have doubted the judgment of a leaping panther as Monteiro's in the saddle. What baffled me was the point of it all. It seemed an eccentric kind of courage. If at least he had been showing off, I could have understood, but he was always alone, and up there I was invisible to him.

I told no one—for one thing, Aunt Amecia would have had a fit, and it would seem that I was snooping and telling tales. When at meal times I glanced surreptitiously at the Captain's austere face, it was hard to reconcile the elderly petty tyrant with the daring, reckless rider at the cliff edge.

One morning the man called Steffan turned up at breakfast time with instructions to show me round the plantations. Amecia had been mentioning only the previous evening that he was the son of a permanent German resident and a local woman. He had formerly been a tourist guide, speaking several languages fluently, and ran the estate virtually single-handed. He appeared in a workaday outfit of native linen shirt, and corduroy trousers tucked into short *Canacheira* boots. An old Panama hat, which he wore with a certain style, crowned his head and completed the effect. Tall and lean, he was probably in his thirties, and his very light eyes contrasted with his swarthy but finely cut features and trim, black moustache.

His English was slightly accented but, unlike the Captain's, quite idiomatic. Ines addressed him in Portuguese, in a querulous tone, and Aunt Amecia cut in with some remark that made him laugh uproariously. Then he turned to me:

"Come along, youngster." He winked. "I hope you're interested in agriculture."

"Poor Jerry!" teased Ines. "Back to school again."

Monteiro had already left. Somehow I could not imagine this conversation taking place in his presence, which seemed to inhibit everyone—esxept, of course, the irrepressible Amecia.

"You must take a hat," she commanded. "The sun is *terrible!*"

"What he needs," said Steffan, "is a mask."

"Good gracious!" laughed my mother. "What on earth for?"

Steffan merely grinned and beckoned to me to go. I felt immediately at ease in his company. Something about his slow, easy movements and crooked half-smile suggested a great capacity for patience—showing me round must have been a waste of his time but he showed no sign of annoyance. As we neared the plantations, the meaning of his reference to a mask became clear; the fertilizers they used stank to high heaven. We trod along dusty lanes flanked by phalanges of purplish sugar cane; acres and acres of land and not a square foot wasted. The flamboyant banana trees were pregnant with green fruit, and in places, where the vine had coiled up an archway of reeds, black bunches of grapes dangled temptingly above my nose. We came across toiling peasants, rough-hewn barefoot men in straw hats, who would straighten their backs to greet me. *"O menino!"* One lopped off a length of sugar cane with a kind of machete, whittled down the bark and offered me the pulp to chew. Steffan laughed as the sticky juice ran down my chin and the fibres lodged between my teeth.

It was rich soil. The estate must have been profitable. At one point we stopped to watch a group irrigating furrowed land. They were lifting a stone slab to let water flow from an artificial duct. And suddenly, heralded by a thumping of hoofs, the Captain burst into the clearing on a horse fit for El Cid Campeador—unmistakably the gray horse I saw him put through its grim paces every morning.

He dismounted with agility, tossed the reins to Steffan and stood, legs wide apart, tapping his thigh with a riding crop and frowning at the laborers. Something about the work seemed to displease him, for he burst into quick-fire Portuguese, aimed partly at Steffan, partly at the group of peasants. One old man, perhaps the foreman, who stood ankle-deep in the mire, doffed his hat and argued respectfully. Monteiro, hardly listening, barked louder, the timbre of his voice growing military. I noticed that Steffan watched him impassively and kept silent. He caught my gaze once and winked with a faint smile—I think he was trying to say that the act was being staged for my benefit. At last the Captain appeared to tire of the argument and, dismissing the old man with a gesture, turned to me.

"Well!" he said. "Looking the place, no? Ver' educative—they teach this in your school, eh?"

"Er . . . yes, sir," I said dubiously.

"Good!" He stretched an arm absently and patted the horse's neck. "You like horses? But, of course, all Englishmen like horses. You must ride mine. Have you ridden before?"

"No, sir," I admitted honestly, "but . . ."

"No matter. There is a first time always. Come!"

Steffan said something too fast for me to catch.

"Nonsense!" snapped Monteiro. "It is perfectly safe."

And without more ado he picked me up and deposited me in the saddle as if I were a piece of luggage. Demonstrating how the reins should be held, he briefly expounded a few elementary rules of riding. Finally, as if quoting from some manual to operate a machine:

"At the end of the pathway is another clearing. Pull at the reins this way or that and he will turn back—off you are, now!"

Gingerly I dug my heels into those powerful flanks, and to my great surprise the huge beast lurched forward obediently. Steffan took hold of the bridle-rein and began to walk alongside.

"Steffan!" Monteiro glared meaningly at his overseer, who stepped back with a shrug and left me on my own.

All my riding experience is contained in that brief episode—I have not been tempted near a horse since. But in that first glorious minute I became Richard the Lion Heart, Tom Mix, and a Don Cossack rolled into one. Then suddenly I began to feel the insecurity of my perch, with my feet barely touching the stirrups. The others were out of sight now, hidden by the tall sugar canes, and my illusion of being in control burst like a bubble. Was it true that horses instantly sensed if their riders were incompetent or afraid? I remembered which particular horse I was on; what if it should take it into its head to break into a gallop and head for the cliff? Steffan had not seemed too happy about leaving me alone. Had the animal a vicious streak? But the horse reached the clearing without so much as a restless snort and, obeying my apologetic pull, tamely went back the way we had come. The Captain, having resumed his argument with the old peasant, took no notice of me. Steffan came and helped me to dismount.

"All right?"

I nodded, smiling bravely, but I suppose he knew I was scared.

Later, after the Captain had left, Steffan took me to see his quarters and I asked him why he had hesitated to leave me by myself on the horse.

He considered the question, with a half amused look. "I don't trust the brute. I have been thrown on more than one occasion while exercising it."

"Has it ever thrown Captain Monteiro?" I was thinking of the risks he took every morning at the cliff-edge, wondering if Steffan was aware of it.

"I doubt it. The Captain is a fine horseman."

"Why. . . ." I fumbled for the right words. "Why should some animals be nasty like that—what's *wrong* with them, I mean?"

"Wrong?" Steffan shrugged. "More or less like people, I suppose. Some inherit the nasty traits; others acquire them. I don't believe there is much really wrong with this horse. High-spirited, perhaps; nothing more. It is the Captain who is wrong—all spur and crop . . . and hate! He wants to prove he is master, *all* the time." He smiled cynically. "I don't mean only with the horse, either. . . ." He eyed me uncertainly, perhaps wondering if he was not being a trifle indiscreet, and changed the conversation.

Steffan's living quarters, a delightful outhouse half smothered by creepers and surrounding vegetation, included an office, a store and a small workshop. The office had an untidy, busy look. A large old mahogany desk stood in the middle, cluttered with papers, files and ledgers.

"There you are." He smiled wryly. "I am—how do you say it—a jack of all crafts? Look!" He opened a window. Outside was a wire-mesh enclosure and some kennels. A beautiful, sleek retriever came bounding up excitedly. "See?" He gestured towards a rack full of sporting guns on the far wall. "I am a sort of gamekeeper as well. Sometimes His Excellency has friends coming from the city for a day's shoot in the hills. And, naturally, as Steffan has nothing better to do, he is expected to organize everything without the slightest hitch."

I need to stand back and view Steffan from a distance of thirty-odd years to get him in perspective. In my youth I looked at pictures too closely, without critical sense. It never struck me then that he was virtually a social outcast, belonging neither to the peasantry nor to the family. He worked, ate and slept alone in his bungalow—and how plain Monteiro made it, in a score of irritating little ways, that he was unwelcome in the house. I only half understood that it was because of Ines, though it was obvious from her conversation that she was attracted by the handsome, well-spoken overseer. And Monteiro missed few opportunities to humiliate him in her presence—in my presence, too, for some adults do not seem to realize how observant are those unobtrusive children. Poor Ines! She was utterly dominated by her father. What I have wondered is why Steffan put up with it. With his innate ability and his languages he could surely have made good elsewhere. Perhaps the Captain knew his worth and paid him well—and knew too how far he could go without running the risk of losing him.

The time for our departure drew near. One morning I awoke to a strange sound I could not immediately place. I rose and peered out of the window, guessing the cause. The weather had been so consistently fine that the gale that was blowing seemed unreal. It shrieked through the trees and howled menacingly round the building. I dressed, went downstairs to breakfast and found the three women discussing what a terrible night it had been. The Captain, as usual, was not at the breakfast table. Aunt Amecia saw me come in and promptly forbade me to go wandering about in such weather, and my mother, who rarely interfered with my boyish activities, mildly endorsed this injunction. After the meal, resigned to spending the morning indoors, I drifted glumly into the library which was crammed with unattractive-looking volumes bound in dark leather. A patient search yielded nothing in the one language I could read, and finally I settled for a slim tome that had some bleak prints of anaemic children in sailor suits.

It was oppressively stuffy in the library. The weather had become hot and close, the pressure of the wind on the house seemed to suffocate. The illustrations conveyed to me a notion of vapid goodness that I rebelled against on principle. I wanted to be outside, feeling the wind; I thought of the violence of the sea, which would be visible from my secret look-out. I put the book aside and peered down the corridor towards the living-room at the front. Amecia and my mother sat between me and the door. But there was another way; the kitchen at the opposite end of the corridor. In a minute I had slipped out unseen.

The first buffeting of the wind shook the lethargy out of me. The mad war dance of the trees, with leaves and catkins flying about like angry living creatures, excited me as I cut across the wood. Tall date palms tossed their heads to the rhythm of a droning melody that rose to a screech and fell again. I caught the distant pounding of the waves against the cliff. Dirty gray clouds came billowing in from the sea. Stunned and awe-struck by this unfamiliar mood of nature, I was almost ready to accept what followed as if it were part of the general confusion.

As I crossed a small clearing, the gray horse, saddled but riderless, its eyes drawn back in a wild look, crashed out of the undergrowth. Instinctively I threw myself flat against a tree trunk as it galloped by, kicking back the earth as it cleared the shrubs on the other side with a perfect leap. The whole thing must have taken about five seconds; just long enough for me to notice a blood-red streak on the horse's flank. For a while I remained pressed against the tree, half expecting the runaway to reappear. Then the full implication of what I had seen dawned on me. Without thinking—that frightful howling in my ears seemed to preclude thought—I started to run. I ran through the thicket, tearing my clothes, and emerged breathless and uncertain of my purpose at the fringe of the wood, where the ground took a downward slope. Perhaps I had expected to see the Captain lying hurt or unconscious on the plain below. There was no one; nothing—only the clouds and the cliff, and the spray of the breakers below drifting inland like a fine mist. A foolish desire to look over the edge filled me and, bent against the wind, I staggered down the hill. Half a dozen yards away from my goal, I threw myself full length on the grass and crawled forward. Perhaps it was the steadying force of the wind that neutralized my fear of heights, for I got as far as craning my neck over the edge. A savage sea gaped momentarily to show a lone sharp rock like a stained tooth, then surged back over it and slammed against the cliff face. I rolled back in time with the swell, for it seemed as if it would envelop me too, and I ran before the wind.

For the first time, a reasonable fear hit me. I could not have been more convinced of the Captain's fate, but would not believe it. Drenched from the spray but hardly aware of it, and driven by childish optimism, I roamed those wind-swept grounds, along the tracks he was likely to have ridden. He could well have fallen on the way—a swinging branch could have hit him, a moment of neglect, the horse might have panicked in the storm; anything. For perhaps an hour I searched in vain. At last I gave up and returned slowly to the house, exhausted but still hopeful.

I shall never forget the scene that I found on arrival. Amid the comings and goings of scared-looking servants, Aunt Amecia was having a fit of hysterics; Ines was quietly weeping in a corner of the great living-room; and my mother, calm but paler than I had ever seen her, was coming towards me as I entered.

"Oh, Jerry!" She put her arm round my shoulders. "I knew you would be all right. You should never have gone out in this weather. Why were you disobedient?"

I had nothing to say. I was too tired and mixed up to explain.

"Never mind, dear." She drew my head towards her. "I'm afraid something terrible has happened."

And, knowing everything, I nodded and asked no questions.

"You're wet through," she said. "You had better go upstairs and change before you catch cold."

Later, I gathered it was Steffan who had found out about the accident and brought the news. He had left immediately for a nearby village to inform the police. He sent word that he had had to accompany the village *guarda* to Funchal to make a formal report of the accident, and I did not see him again before we left. We had been due to leave in a couple of weeks, but my mother decided to take the first ship home, while Amecia stayed on to keep Ines company.

Early the following year, Aunt Amecia died in Lisbon, and that ended our contact with the Portuguese branch of the family. My memory of the incident, starved of reminders, grew weak as the years sped by. Then came the war, and the new fast-changing world that pushed our old one into history before its proper time.

He leaned against the bar, still seeming uncertain whether my unexpected company was agreeable to him, still peering into his glass as if some rare insect had fallen into the liquor. At last he made up his mind.

"I am sorry," he said. "I am not being very polite, am I?"

I brushed aside his apologies. "Let me buy you a drink."

"Well, why not? I will have another Scotch, if you please." He made it sound as if that "another" would be his second; his eyes suggested it might be his twelfth.

"Are you living here in London," I said tentatively, "or on business, perhaps?"

"Neither." He paused to toss back his drink. "There is something wrong with me. I went to see a specialist in Lisbon, but I did not like his verdict. A friend recommended a good man here."

"Oh, I'm sorry to hear that. Was he . . . er . . . a little more encouraging?"

He smiled a shadow of his crooked smile, jerking his chin towards the empty tumbler on the bar. "As you can see, I am still building up courage to make an appointment."

"Perhaps you're being over pessimistic."

"Let's talk about something else," he said quite civilly. "I will buy *you* a drink now." He signalled to the barman. "Tell me, have you been to Madeira recently?"

"No, not since that time. You still live there, I suppose?"

"Of course."

"I wonder . . . is the daughter still living, do you know?"

"You mean Ines? She is my wife."

"Well! I feel I should congratulate you, but it seems a little late for that, doesn't it?"

He chuckled. "Thank you, all the same."

"You know, I still remember when her father was killed in that accident. Must have been quite a shock for her."

He frowned. "Ah, yes; most unfortunate—have another Scotch."

"You've just ordered two."

"I have?"

The barman came up at that moment and refilled our glasses. Steffan stared dully and seemed to lose himself in his thoughts.

I tried to bring him back. "I've often wondered, did they ever find the body?"

"Eh? The body?" He considered for a moment, then shook his head. "The Atlantic is very big. The sharks would not have left much of it, anyway."

"He was a bit foolhardy, wasn't he?"

"Foolhardy? He was insane, that man. He used to boast to me he could walk his mount a foot away from the edge of that cliff. And he did, too."

"He was a jolly good horseman, I remember. I never really thought it could happen."

"It had to happen. That morning the horse must have stumbled on a hole. I found it lying there with both front legs broken—had to shoot it on the spot."

He fell silent, and his look became distant and morose. Somehow, I could think of nothing else to say. In a while he offered me his hand and, excusing himself, hoped we might meet again. He was not specific as to where or when, and I did not press him. I never saw him again.

I used to lose sleep over not being able to reconcile what he had told me about the horse with what I saw with my own eyes. Unless I had dreamt my piece, he was lying, and there is something disturbing about a lie in such circumstances. Lately I have come to accept the whole thing as one more addition to life's many uncertainties. Whatever happened, happened too long ago to matter any longer.

E.G. Chipulina is a Gibraltarian, an accountant, who has been writing and publishing short stories for more than 15 years.

"The deathly hush in the passage
suddenly became so strident that it could have been
called screaming deathly hush.
It appeared I was on to something."

A Case
of Immaculate Conception

BY AUSTIN COATES

Fun and frustration in court.

I cannot resist telling this one.

The court was rather more full than usual, most of the adult members of two families having come in. The two families were neighbors, living in a rather ramshackle, but fairly solid, row of wooden shop-houses in a congested part of industrial Tsuen Wan. Technically they were squatters, and the area was one of those we hoped eventually to see pulled down to make way for modern apartment blocks.

They were single-story structures. In most of them, the shop section fronted the street; further in was the sleeping area, flimsily compartmented for various members of the family; after this came the kitchen and washing places, and a small rear yard, filled with the astonishing ragbag collections which Chinese of this type amass as some obscure part of their instinct for survival.

The complainant family had a daughter, aged about eighteen

and still unmarried, who was in the unfortunate position of expecting a baby; and her parents had come to demand that I order the twenty-year-old son of the neighboring family to marry their daughter without delay, since, they alleged, he was the unborn baby's father.

The defendant family said that this allegation was preposterous nonsense, that their son had never had anything to do with the girl, and that they refused to be browbeaten in this disgraceful way, their son accused of immorality. There was no question of his marrying the girl, and there never had been. They scarcely knew their neighbors anyway, and their son had never even spoken to the girl.

The boy and the girl were present. Inhibited somewhat by their parents, who were doing most of the talking, they were both pleasant types. The boy worked in a factory; the girl worked at home making plastic handbags.

"Do you confirm what your father says, that you've never spoken to this girl?" I asked.

He confirmed it.

I turned to the girl's father.

"But you are suggesting that this is untrue," I said. "You are suggesting that your daughter has, in fact, spoken to this young man."

The girl's father was truculent. He didn't know whether his daughter had spoken to the boy or not. What he did know was that this was the young man who had interfered with his daughter.

"And are you saying, too, that you have never spoken to this young man?" I inquired of the girl.

She lowered her eyes, and would not reply.

"But you insist that he is the father of your baby?" I pursued.

She was silent for a long time. She had flushed, eyes always downcast.

"Yes," she whispered at last.

"Listen, young man," I said to the boy, "are you quite sure you're telling me the truth? Isn't there something else you *could* tell me, if your parents were not here—something you would prefer them not to know?"

Eyes downcast on his side too, his pale face gave no indication of a reaction. But my remarks produced a protest from his parents. Their son had nothing to conceal, they insisted. They knew the position. The other family's allegation was totally without foundation.

"Are you sure," I went on, addressing the boy, "that you haven't met this girl somewhere outside?"

"No! Of course he hasn't!" shouted both his parents simultaneously.

"No," replied the boy, quietly and quite plainly.

It sounded like the truth.

I addressed myself to the girl's father.

"I must tell you frankly, I find it difficult to deal with this complaint of yours. What you are saying about this young man is a very grave accusation. You cannot expect me to believe it, or even listen to it, unless you can produce some facts to substantiate it."

"I have facts!" he retorted hotly.

"Well—?"

"In the shower!" he snapped out.

"I beg your pardon?" I inquired, vaguely wondering where there might be a shower in our office.

"Yes," he said. "In the shower! That's where!"

I cupped my chin in my hands.

"What shower? Where?"

"In my house!"

"Oh! I understand!" I exclaimed; then, finding that I didn't, added, "No, I'm afraid I don't understand. What do you really mean?"

"When she takes a *shower!*" the wretched father shouted at me, almost overcome by my inability to understand.

"When she takes a shower," I repeated slowly. "Where *is* the shower?"

From my office one was always distantly aware of the bustle and noise in the other parts of the building; and at this moment I wondered why it was that I should have suddenly thought about this. Then it occurred to me. There were surprisingly few sounds from the rest of the building. There was, in fact—apart from the distant bustle of Kowloon—almost silence. There was, now I came to pay keener attention to the matter, more than silence. There was what is known behind the scenes in the London theatre as "deathly hush," which is a kind of indrawing of breath (accompanied by tiptoes and craned heads) so absolutely silent as to be painfully audible.

I did not have to be told. All work in the outer offices had stopped, while every member of the staff who considered himself sufficiently senior to do so had silently crept up the passage, where, just out of sight from the open door of my office, the lot of them had assembled, poised, listening to every word with bated breath.

"Where is the shower?" I repeated steadily, trying hard to control myself from yelling at the staff to go back to their work.

The shower, it appeared, was at the back of the house. With a projecting cover of some sort, it was external to the building, situated in the back yard, and modestly screened.

"You mean," I said, "that it is possible to pass from your back yard to your neighbor's?"

Certainly not! came the almost injured reply. There was a strong plank wall between the two yards, and it was impossible to pass.

"Then what do you mean? Where does the shower come into it?"

"He *saw* her!" the girl's father shouted at me desperately.

"I see. You mean, realizing she was having a shower, he managed to climb over the plank wall, and . . ." Modesty forbade the rest.

But the poor father only looked more desperate than ever.

"He *saw* her!" he repeated, with even greater emphasis.

This was becoming too much for the Special Magistrate.

"Look here, my dear man," I said reasonably, "you are not, I hope, trying to tell me that if a young man chances to see a young girl having a shower, this causes the girl to make a baby. Or are you?"

From the youngsters there was silence. From the four parents there was a unanimous snort of disgust at finding they had journeyed all this way to be heard by a magistrate who asked such ridiculous questions.

"*He* doesn't understand," the father muttered contemptuously to my interpreter, using an off-hand word to describe me.

"No, he certainly doesn't!" I replied sharply, before the interpreter had time to translate. "If you have a genuine grievance against this family, or against this young man, why do you not tell me what it is?"

It seemed to me that their accusation against the boy was a cover, shielding the real cause of their animosity towards the other family. This real cause was evidently something quite different. But how to discover what it was?

There was silence.

"Well, I'm sorry," I said, "but if that is all you can produce to substantiate your statement I'm afraid my answer must be that this young man has no case to answer."

With triumphant looks and inaudible sniffs, the boy's parents turned their backs on the other parents, who remained silent, the girl's father staring at me with the helplessness an intelligent man evinces when trying to explain something to an ignoramus.

"Listen to me," I said to him, by this time almost in my own self-defense. "You have all more or less agreed that this young man has never spoken to your daughter. He may once have seen her taking her bath—perhaps you should make that plank wall higher. Your daughter must go out sometimes on her own. How do you know that she doesn't have some other boy friend, whom you know nothing about?"

They dismissed this out of hand. Their daughter did not go out on her own.

"Then, what you are telling me is that this young man, by having set eyes on your daughter when she was naked, has caused her to conceive a child."

All of them rustled about for a moment—Western magistrates, it seemed to them, had strange ideas—and then the girl's father muttered under his breath to the interpreter:

"Can't he understand? At *night!*"

"At night?" I queried. "You mean, your daughter is in the habit of taking a shower at night?"

In the passage outside, there was a sudden renewed outburst of deathly hush. It evidenced the fact that the only person in the office who did *not* know what this case was about was the Special Magistrate, the game being to see how long it would take him to find out. They may even have been laying bets on it.

No, certainly not! came the reply to my query. The girl did *not* take a bath at night.

"Then what has night go to do with it?" I asked. "Where *are* you all usually at night? Sleeping, I presume."

Yes. They were sleeping.

"Well, where do you sleep?"

It appeared that the sleeping quarters in both houses were approximately adjacent, that both front and back doors were securely locked before everyone went to sleep, and that there was no possibility of anyone passing from one house to the other, or going outside, without waking someone up.

I had reached the end of this line of questioning, and it had led nowhere. But being for the moment at a loss to know what to ask them next, and being unwilling to show them I was lost, with wearied obstinacy I pursued the same line a little further, all the while thinking hard what really salient question to raise next.

"And where exactly do you sleep?" I asked the girl in a bored way.

She slept in the same bed as her mother.

"And where do you sleep?" I inquired of the boy.

He slept alone.

It was meaningless to pursue the matter, but I went on listlessly.

"Whereabouts do you have your bed?"

His bed was against the wall.

"Which wall?"

It was the wall of the other shop-house.

The deathly hush in the passage suddenly became so strident that it could have been called screaming deathly hush. It appeared I was on to something.

I addressed the girl's mother.

"And just where is your bed situated?"

Her bed too was against a wall—the wall of the other shop-house.

"And you say your daughter shares your bed with you?"

"Yes."

"Which—er"—it was difficult to know how to word it—"which of you sleeps on the room side of your bed?"

"I do," the mother replied.

"I see. So your daughter sleeps on the wall side?"

"Yes."

The wall was of wood, and perhaps a knotch had fallen out of it. Anyway, somewhere—and at just about the right place—there was a hole in it.

Not a very big hole. But just big enough.

This case occurred in my third year as magistrate, when I should have known better than to have kept those six people in such prolonged embarrassment. I say all six were embarrassed, because, as the reader, who is by this time becoming accustomed to the happenings in a Chinese court, will already have realized, the boy's parents, despite the attitudes they struck, were fully aware of what had happened. There was even a moment (when they swung themselves away from the other parents) when they thought that, with such an idiot of a magistrate, they were going to get away with it—because they did not really wish their son to marry, considering him to be too young.

Perhaps it was particularly hot and humid that morning—I can't remember—but anyway, I was extremely slow in the uptake, since I was not paying attention to the euphemisms being employed. In no language is euphemism used more than in Chinese, and on no subject are there more Chinese euphemisms than in anything pertaining to sex. Coarsenesses apart—and the Chinese language has its fair share of these—it would almost be true to say that sex, if it is ever mentioned at all in speech, can only be mentioned in euphemistic terms. The very word for sex—the secret thing—is a euphemism.

In what the girl's father was saying to me, the shower in the backyard had nothing to do with it. For "shower" read "naked," for "saw" read "touched," and it will be seen that the father was making a completely explicit statement: "When she was naked, he touched her in the night." He could not be more explicit without using unprintable words.

And there the six of them had sat, in acute embarrassment, because for some reason that morning I was too slow-witted to grasp it.

This is a story which, I think, gives an idea of the difficulties involved in understanding what goes on around one in a Chinese society. To appreciate how silly a foreigner can be in China, it is almost worth glancing at the dialogue of the case a second time, this time suffering with the two Chinese families, instead of struggling with the magistrate.

But to the reader who wishes to do this, let me first explain why they had come. What had happened was too shameful for the boy's parents to admit—the entire family would have lost face— and this had created a socially impossible situation, which the two families themselves could not resolve, and which could *never* be the basis of a marriage alliance. Once again, as with the case in which the magistrate outrivalled the wisdom of Solomon, authority was needed to put things right.

Very gently and kindly, the Special Magistrate inquired of the young couple whether they would like to start talking to each other—because it was true, they never had—and Mr. Lo, reading my meaning from my tone of voice, skilfully slipped my words into the perfect Chinese euphemism, behind which lay the implication, "Would you like to get married?"

Both smiled, and said they would; and the suggestion having come from so exalted a source, all question of shame was removed.

They all departed in a comparatively amiable state—I say comparatively, because none of the four parents had really yet recovered from the shock of discovering that they had produced offspring of quite such exceptional agility.

Austin Coates has worked and lived in Asia since 1944 and is the author of several books about the area.

"Kite-flying was then the sport of kings . . ."

The Kite-Maker

BY RUSKIN BOND

**Beautifully told, the story brings to mind
the line from William Butler Yeats: "When you are
old and grey and full of sleep . . ."**

THERE was but one tree in the street known as Gali Ram Nath—
an ancient banyan which had grown through the cracks of an
abandoned mosque—and little Ali's kite had caught in its
branches.

The boy, barefoot and clad only in a torn shirt, ran along the
cobbled stones of the narrow street to where his grandfather sat
nodding dreamily in the sunshine of their back courtyard.

"Grandfather!" shouted the boy. "The kite has gone!"

The old man woke from his daydream with a start, and raising
his head, displayed a beard which would have been white had it
not been dyed red with mehndi leaves.

"Did the twine break?" he asked. "I know that kite-twine is not
what it used to be."

"No, grandfather, the kite is stuck in the banyan tree."

The old man chuckled. "You have yet to learn how to fly a kite properly, my child. And I am too old to teach you, that's the pity of it. But you shall have another." He had just finished making a new kite from bamboo, paper and thin silk, and it lay in the sun, firming up. It was a pale pink kite, with a small green tail. The old man handed it to Ali, and the boy raised himself on his toes and kissed his grandfather's hollowed-out cheek.

"I will not lose this one," he said. "This kite will fly like a bird." And he turned on his heels and skipped out of the courtyard.

The old man remained dreaming in the sun. His kite-shop had gone. The premises long since sold to a junk-dealer but he still made kites for his own amusement and for the benefit of his grandson, Ali. Not many people bought kites in these days of rockets and sputniks. Adults disdained them, and children preferred to spend their money at the movies. Moreover, there were few open spaces left for the flying of kites. The city had swallowed up the green maidan which had stretched from the old fort walls to the river bank.

But the old man remembered a time when grown men flew kites from the maidan, and great battles were fought, the kites swerving and swooping in the sky, tangling with each other, until the string of one was cut. Then the defeated but liberated kite would float away into the blue unknown. There was a good deal of betting, and money frequently changed hands.

Kite-flying was then the sport of kings, and the old man remembered how the Nawab himself would come down to the riverbank with his retinue, and join in this noble pastime. There was time in those days to spend an idle hour with a gay, dancing strip of paper. Now everyone hurried, hurried in a heat of hope, and delicate things like kites and daydreams were trampled underfoot.

He, Mahmood the kite-maker, had in the prime of his life been well-known throughout the city. Some of his more elaborate kites sold for as much as three or four rupees. Upon the request of the Nawab he had once made a very special kind of kite, unlike any that had been seen in the district. It consisted of a series of small, very light paper discs, trailing on a thin bamboo frame.

To the extremity of each disc he fixed a sprig of grass, forming a balance on both sides. The surface of the foremost disc was slightly convex, and a fantastic face was painted on it, having two eyes made of small mirrors. The discs, decreasing in size from head to tail, assumed an undulatory form, and gave the kite the appearance of a crawling serpent. It required great skill to raise this cumbersome device from the ground, and only Mahmood could manage it.

Everyone had of course heard of the "Dragon Kite" that Mahmood had built, and word went round that it possessed supernatural powers. A large crowd assembled on the maidan to watch its first public launching in the presence of the Nawab. At the first attempt it refused to leave the ground. The discs made a plaintive, protesting sound, and the sun was trapped in the little mirrors and made of the kite a living, complaining creature.

And then the wind came from the right direction, and the Dragon Kite soared into the sky, wriggling its way higher and higher, with the sun still glinting in its devil-eyes. And when it went very high, it pulled fiercely on the twine, and Mahmood's young sons had to help him with the reel; but still the kite pulled, determined to be free, to break loose, to live a life of its own. And eventually it did so.

The twine snapped, the kite leapt away toward the sun, sailed on heavenward until it was lost to view. It was never found again, and Mahmood wondered afterwards if he had made too vivid, too living a thing of the great kite. He did not make another like it, but instead he presented the Nawab with a musical kite, one that made a sound like the veena when it rose in the air.

Yes, those were more leisurely, more spacious days. But the Nawab had died years ago, and his descendants were almost as poor as Mahmood himself. Kite-makers, like poets, once had their patrons; but no one knew Mahmood now, or asked his name and occupation, simply because there were too many people in the Gali, and nobody could be bothered about neighbors.

When he was younger and had fallen sick, everyone in the neighborhood had come to ask after his health; but now, when his days were drawing to a close, no one visited him. True, most of his old friends were dead; his sons had grown up, one was working in a local garage, the other had been in Pakistan at the time of partition and could not now rejoin his relatives.

The children who had bought kites from him ten years ago, they were grown men, struggling for a living; they did not have time for the old man and his memories. They had grown up in a swift-changing, competitive world, and looked at the old kite-maker with the same indifference as they looked at the banyan tree.

Both were taken for granted as permanent fixtures that were of no concern to the raucous, sweating mass of humanity that surrounded them. No longer did people gather under the banyan tree to discuss their problems and their plans: only in the summer months did someone seek shelter under it from the fierce sun.

But there was of course the boy, his grandson. . . . It was good that his son worked close by, and the daughter-in-law could live with him. It gladdened his heart to watch the boy at play in the winter sunshine, growing under his eyes like a young and well-nourished sapling, putting forth new leaves each day.

There is a great affinity between trees and men. We grow at much the same pace, if we are no hurt or starved or cut down. In our youth we are resplendent creatures, and in our declining years we stoop a little, we remember, we stretch our brittle limbs in the sun, and, with a sigh, shed our last leaves.

Mahmood was like the banyan, his hands gnarled and twisted like the roots of the ancient tree. Ali was like the young mimosa planted at the end of the courtyard. In two years both he and the tree would acquire the strength and confidence of their early youth.

The voices in the street grew fainter, and Mahmood wondered if he was going to fall asleep and dream, as he so often did, of a kite so beautiful and powerful that it would resemble the great white bird of the Hindus, Garuda, God Vishnu's famous steed. He would like to make a wonderful new kite for little Ali. He had nothing else to leave the boy.

He heard Ali's voice in the distance, but did not realize that the boy was calling to him. The voice seemed to come from very far away.

Ali was at the courtyard door, asking if his mother had as yet returned from the bazaar. When Mahmood did not answer, the boy came forward, repeating his question. The sunlight was slanting across the old man's head, and a small white butterfly was perched on his flowing beard. Mahmood was silent; and when Ali put his small brown hand on the old man's shoulder, he met with no response. The boy heard a faint sound, like the rubbing of marbles in his pocket.

Suddenly afraid, Ali turned and moved to the door, and then ran down the street shouting for his mother.

The butterfly left the old man's beard and flew to the mimosa tree. And in the banyan tree, a sudden gust of wind caught the torn kite and lifted it into the air, carrying it far above the struggling, sweating city, into the azure-blue sky.

Ruskin Bond's moving story "The Garlands on His Brow"
appeared in SSI No. 5. Born and bred in India, Mr. Bond spent
several years in England where his first book, The Room on the
Roof, *was published. It brought him the John Llewellyn Rys Prize.*
He returned to India as a free-lance writer and has published short
stories, poems, children's books and a biography of Jawaharlal
Nehru. A Girl From Copenhagen *is his latest collection of short*
stories.

"... looking again, he saw that it was a window in the house of Sarah Leah, the widow."

The Celebrants

BY S.Y. AGNON

**A Passover courting in Biblical rhythm
dappled by earthy humor.**

THERE are many who have heard the tale of Reb Mechel, the beadle, and the wealthy Sarah Leah. At the same time there are as many who have not heard it; and for those who have not heard it, it is worth the telling.

This is the tale of Mechel, the beadle. When Mechel, the beadle, left the House of Study on the first night of Passover his mood was cheerful. Blessed be Thy Name, said he to himself, that the Eve of Passover is over and done with so that I too can rejoice this night like other folk. But when he had locked the doors and found himself proceeding homeward his good mood left him. He knew that he went to no royal feasting hall but to a tumble-down dwelling; that he would be sitting not on a fine handsome couch but on a torn cushion unmended by woman's hand; and that he must trouble himself a great deal to warm his food. For at the time, Mechel, the beadle, was a widower; there was no woman in his home to prepare his table, make his bed or cook his meals. Truth to tell, many householders had wished to invite him to celebrate the Passover feast with them. Reb Mechel, they said, tonight the whole world is rejoicing and all Israel feasts with their households, so why should you celebrate on your own? Be happy, Reb Mechel, that the demons have no power on this night; but even so there is a peril of sadness, which is as much prohibited on the Passover as leaven, the Merciful One deliver us. Yet Mechel refused all offers of hospitality, for he did not wish to burden another's table at the festival.

The streets had emptied, and all the houses of the town shone with Passover light. The moon was bright and gracious, and a spring breeze blew. Mechel began to turn his mind away from himself and enjoy the wonders of the Creation, jingling the keys of the synagogue like a bell. But hearing the sound of the keys he grew sorrowful and began to remind himself bitterly how he was the beadle of the House of Study, toiling hard and doing all sorts of work; and how, when he had completed his work and returned home, he remained cramped and lonely between the walls, never even tasting cooked food; since if he put food on to warm he would be asleep before it was cooked. So he would stay his hunger with an onion roll or some bread and radish, or the potato a woman might bring to the House of Study so that he would pray for the souls of her dear ones to rest in peace. But what you may do all the year round, and rest satisfied, you may not do on a festival when we are bidden to rejoice.

On the way home he noticed that one house had a window open; looking again, he saw that it was a window in the house of Sarah Leah, the widow. She herself was standing at the window looking out. Mechel bowed to her with the greeting, "Festivals for joy, Sarah Leah."

"Holidays and appointed times for gladness, Reb Mechel," responded Sarah Leah. "Whence and whither, Reb Mechel?"

"I am coming from the House of Study," said Mechel, "on my way home to prepare my table and sit and celebrate."

Sarah Leah nodded her head and sighed. I see she would like to say something to me, said Mechel to himself, and stood waiting.

Seeing Mechel standing waiting, she said, "I just opened my window to see if it were time to leave, for I am celebrating at my neighbor's. I've prepared all sorts of good things, by your life, and I'm short of nothing in order to celebrate the Passover down to the last detail, and all the same I have to go leave my own home and burden myself on others. It is not enough that I go burdening them every Sabbath and festival, when I suddenly appear among them for the Hallowing and the Havdala; I have to go bothering them on Passover as well."

"Well, it may be a bother in your eyes," said Mechel, "but others regard it as fulfilling a commandment."

"A commandment, d'you say, Reb Mechel?" responded Sarah Leah. "Do you suppose such commandments come easily to those who perform them? Here's a man who's busy all day long and never sees his wife and children; Passover comes, a time of rest, he wishes to sit quiet with his family when in jumps that widow all of a sudden and sits down among them. May it be His Will that I shouldn't sin with my words, the years grow less and the world grows wearier and weaker. In time gone by a Jew would bring any number of guests home with him and there'd be room enough; and nowadays there's no room even for a lonely widow like me. I remember Passover at Father's, may he rest in peace, when we'd have ten Jews and more there. And was my husband, may he rest in peace, accustomed to celebrate Passover without a guest? And I have to leave my home now. And am I short of anything here? If it's wine a body wants, here's wine and enough to spare for an extra glass; and if its matzoth, here are the extra special matzoth; if it's meat, here's a turkey cock whose wings were absolutely hidden by fat.

"Why, what did the neighbors say, 'Sarah Leah, don't tie him to the foot of your bed or he'll drag you across Sambayton River.' That's no bird, that's an aurochs. But as long as a woman's in her husband's home, it's all worth while; and once he's dead even the whole of the world isn't worth while. At first I thought of inviting a guest only folks would say, 'That old woman's a fiend from Hell, wants a man for to serve her well.' "

Mechel smiled, sighed and quoted the Talmud, " 'Tis better to dwell in trouble than to dwell in widowhood."

And although the saying was in Aramaic, a tongue Sarah Leah did not understand, she nodded her head like a person saying, "You said it well and true." Mechel's an upright man and assuredly has some good thought in mind. And she added, "There's everything here, but if there's no master in the house what is there in the house? I often ask myself, Sarah Leah, what are you doing here and whom have you here? I have reared children to their full size and they forsook me, so now I am bereft and forsaken, as a table after a feast. I thought of ascending to the Land of Israel to be near the holy places, and not be thinking all the time of my loneliness; but then how can a woman go alone to a place where she is not known? All Israel are brethren, but nevertheless my heart troubles me at the thought of ascending alone."

Mechel felt full of pity for her. He took hold of his right earlock and wished to say words of comfort to her. Yet he could get nothing out, began stammering and at last said, "Woman, is my luck any greater than yours? You, God be praised, are adorned as a bride and eat fine food, while I am chidden and mourning as a widower. But no man in Israel has other to depend on than the loving kindness of the Holy and Blest One. What has any living person to grumble at? The festival should not be degraded."

And from seeking to comfort her he began to feel sorry for himself and he said, "And what is a man? Something bare in the waste. Blessed be He that did not make me a woman. Blessed be His Name that I know how to hallow the wine and prepare for the Passover according to the law. But now go to a tumbledown dwelling and warm up half-cooked food and sit on a broken bed, and then sit on a torn cushion and think you're like a king. It was with good reason that the *Yalkut says,* 'All sufferings are hard to bear, but those of poverty are hardest of all; all sufferings come, and once they are gone leave things as they were; but poverty dims the eyes of a man.' I'm only saying this to balance your saying, 'I'm a woman.' And what's more, the Holy and Blest One has brought a bad cough upon me, may you never know its like, which takes away my breath and steals the life from me and will drive me out of the world." Before he finished speaking he had begun coughing.

"Reb Mechel," said Sarah Leah to him, "don't stand out in the cold; winter may have gone but it's still chilly. Better come into the house and not stand about in the open."

Mechel bowed his head between his shoulders, entered and found himself in a fine dwelling with handsomely decked cushions to recline upon, and a table covered with silverware in the middle of the room, and a bottle of wine on the table, candles burning in all the candlesticks and every corner of the room gleaming and shining with festival. His first words were in honor of the place, for he said, "How fine this room is, where the hands of a woman have been employed." Sarah Leah at once rushed to show him all she had ready for the table. Matzoth and bitter herbs lay there, parsley and haroseth, eggs and a sheepshank and flesh and fish and a fat pudding and borsht, red as wine.

"And who," said Sarah Leah to Mechel, "needs all this array? I'm just about to go off and bother somebody else, but it's hard for me to forget that I'm a housewife, so I prepared a Passover for myself as though my husband were still here and he and I were celebrating like all other folk."

Mechel's heart warmed within him, and he wished to say something, but a furious fit of coughing overcame him. Sarah Leah stared at him with her two eyes and said, "Don't eat too much bitter herbs and don't eat sharp foods, Reb Mechel; you cough too badly. You know what you need? It's a glass of hot tea you need. But who have you at home to make something hot? Wait a few minutes and I'll put the kettle on for you."

But scarce had she finished her sentence when she struck herself on the mouth, crying, "What a silly head I have, to forget that we have to hallow the festival first. Maybe you'll celebrate here?" And since the thought had found expression in the words she repeated, "Maybe you'll celebrate here?"

Mechel saw all the goodness of the housewife and could not move, as though his limb were fastened to the spot where he stood. He began stammering and swallowed his indistinct answer. And Sarah Leah began preparing the feast as had been her wont when her husband was still with her.

So Mechel took the keys of the House of Study and put them away somewhere, staring meanwhile at the white cushions that Sarah Leah had prepared for reclining on during the celebration as though the High Light shone from them. Within a few moments he had let himself down among them, by reason of the thought that the woman would again ask him to celebrate with her. When she saw him at his ease she filled a glass of wine. With one eye on the wine and one on the household ware, he thought to himself, "What a fine spot this is, where a woman's hands do the tending." While thinking, he found the glass of wine at his hand, and his lips of themselves began repeating the hallowing of the wine.

Sarah Leah sighed with satisfaction; her face grew bright; her clothes were suddenly filled with her body, as happens with a rejoicing person; and she thought to herself, "How fine is a Jew's voice when he utters holy words." And within a moment she had brought him a ewer of water. He washed his hands, took a leaf of greenstuff, dipped it in salt water, broke the matzoth in half, put one half in a cloth and hid it away for dessert, lifted up the dish and began reciting, "This is the bread of affliction, that which our fathers ate in the Land of Egypt."

And Sarah Leah wondered at herself, saying, "Just a little while ago I was preparing to leave my house, and now here am I sitting at home?" And she watched Mechel's hand, observing how accustomed his hands were in holy things, until her face grew red and she lowered her eyes in shame. Then she filled the glasses afresh and uncovered the matzoth. Mechel made her a sign. Sarah Leah blushed, dropped her eyes to the prayer book and recited the Four Questions to their close, "This night we all do recline."

Thereupon Mechel set the dishes back in place and repeated in a loud and joyful voice, "We were the slaves of Pharaoh in Egypt"; and he continued reciting the Relation of the Departure from Egypt as far as the feast, interpreting to her in Yiddish all that required interpretation and seasoning the entire Relations with parables and tales of wonder. His sufferings and troubles far from him, his head resting on the cushion, sweat caressing his earlocks and the cushion growing deeper beneath him, he continued. His blood beat through his limbs and his heart might have leapt forth;

a single hour here was preferable to his whole life in This World.

The Order of Passover came to its appointed end. The whole town was silent; the moon spread a canopy of light over the house of Sarah Leah. Mechel tunefully sang, "May His House soon be built," and Sarah Leah responded, "Speedily, speedily, in our own day soon." From the other houses of the street came the chorus, "God rebuild, God rebuild Thy House soon." And the fantasy that is root and branch of Man led them to imagine that here was a strip of the Land of Israel, and they were calmly and happily singing the Song of Songs.

The night passed. The morning birds rose to repeat their portions of song. In the home of Sarah Leah could be heard the voice of a man chanting the Song of Songs.

> *"Here ends the tale of Mechel,*
> *On whom God did bestow*
> *The wealthy lady Mistress*
> *Sarah Leah, the widow."*

Described as a genius and the winner of the Nobel Prize for Literature in 1966, S.Y. Agnon's novels and short stories concentrate on Jews in East Europe and Israel. His work is marked by wit, wisdom and patterns of epic literature. His story "Discourseth of Weighty Matters" appeared in SSI No. 12.

"I just cannot imagine why the Maori
in my class are so hopeless. I am beginning to doubt
if they possess any intelligence at all."

Catching Up

BY WITI IHIMAERA

**No rose petals cover his path
to a college degree . . . but this Maori has
a determined mother!**

WELL what do you know, he'd finally made it! Incredible as it seemed he, Jimmy Jackson Heremaia, could now have letters after his name. Bachelor of Arts. Wow!

And when he considered it, he didn't look so bad in his capping rags after all. He'd thought the black gown with its pink hood would look stupid on him, as if he wasn't meant to wear it. At least it hid his big feet, these feet that had stumbled and tripped him on his way to his degree. The stumbling and tripping were over now. In a few hours' time he'd be walking up that aisle in the town hall and he'd shake the University Chancellor's hand and it would all be over.

Yes, and who cared that it had taken him six years to get his degree! Who gave a damn that he'd just managed to scrape through each of his units! Nobody, that's who!

Jimmy grinned to himself and saw his teeth grinning back from the mirror. He felt like a huge black and pink balloon almost ready to burst. Then, in the corner of the mirror, he saw his father watching him.

—How's it, Batman, Dad winked.

Jimmy gathered his cape and pride around him and sniffed scornfully.

—You don't look so hot yourself, Dad.

His father shrugged and elbowed his son away from the mirror. He saw a hired suit standing there, topped with a bow tie and bottomed with brown shoes painted black for his son's grand occasion. Aue. Nobody would be looking at him, anyway. He put an arm round Jimmy.

—I'm proud of you, son. Really proud. It might have taken you a long time to get your degree, your mother and I might have thought you were a dead loss, but you did it, ay. You got there in the end. I guess we're lucky you got there at all. Boy, you were a dumb kid!

—That's because I inherited *your* brains, ay Dad.

His father punched him playfully.

—If you had my brains you would have finished your degree a long time ago, he said.

—You'd be joking, Dad.

—Never mind. At least you got there. Congratulations, son. About time!

Dad laughed and punched Jimmy again. Then a voice called from the other room.

—Sam? Sam Heremaia? Come here!

Jimmy poked his father in the ribs.

—The boss is calling you, Dad.

His father sighed.

—Your mother and her damn girdle, he mumbled. All right, all right, I'm coming, I'm coming!

Jimmy grinned as his father left the room. Poor Dad. Come to think of it, poor Jimmy too, if Mum wanted him to try for Master of Arts. The trouble with Mum was she didn't know when to give in. Well, if she thought he was going to stay on at university she had another think coming. No matter what she wanted, after tonight it was goodbye to the academic life!

—And why, James Jackson Heremaia, didn't you get that awful hair of yours cut?

Mum. Standing at the door, hitching up her stockings.

—It's not that long, Mum.

—Too long for me! Mum answered. All bristly too. Soon fix that though. Where's the basin! Where's the scissors!

—Oh no you don't, Mum.

She smiled tenderly at him.

—No, I suppose not, son. All those basin cuts I used to give you, you remember them? Those days, all finished with now. But you could have gotten your hair cut just a bit shorter, couldn't you? Just for me? When we walk into the town hall, people will think you're a golliwog!

She came up to him and poked at his hair. It sprang back and snarled at her.

—Golliwog or not, you've made me proud, son. Made us all proud. Your sisters, your brothers, your relations, all of us.

She kissed him and he put his arms round her.

—I finally made it, ay Mum?

—Yes, son. But you sure took your time about it. Here am I, been waiting all these years to show off and you're three years overdue! I'm three years older than I thought I would be and . . .

—You look beautiful, Mum.

—Course I'm beautiful!

—All those professors will be giving you the glad eye tonight, ay Mum.

—Yeah, and I'll be giving it to them too if they do. With my fist!

Mum started to giggle. Suddenly, there was a knock at the door. Jimmy opened it.

—Mister Heremaia? Telegram for you.

—Thanks, Jimmy answered.

He opened the envelope. Mum peered over his shoulder to see who the telegram was from.

—Nosey! Jimmy grinned.

Then his mouth curved into an affectionate smile.

—What does it say? Mum asked.

Jimmy gave her the telegram to read.

CONGRATULATIONS TO OUR MAORI SON FROM HIS PAKEHA
FAMILY ON THE OTHER SIDE OF THE FENCE.
                    LOVE JACK AND SALLY SIMMONS

—That Jack Simmons always knew you would make it, Mum
said. But like us, he didn't think it would take you this long!

She looked at her watch. Dad came into the room, holding
coats in his hands.

—Yes, Mum continued. We better be off. Me and Dad been
traveling all day from Gisborne to this cold place to see you get
graduated, son. We better get down to that town hall before they
change their minds, ay.

Arm in arm, the three of them swept out of the room.

From the top of the hill above Wainuiomata, emerald lights
stretched erratically in the darkness, off-shoots from the broad
Milky Way band between Wellington City and the Hutt Valley.
Around the inner harbor the lights curved like an avenue leading
to the town hall.

Jimmy looked out the window of the car. Bachelor of Arts, what
a joke. Him, of all people. But he wasn't going to be smug about
it. The truth was that it has been no joke at all, his getting this far.

Right from the beginning, getting educated had seemed like a
marathon most of the other kids had already begun while he was
still approaching the starting line. Even then they seemed to have
the right equipment—track shoes, good coaching and the encouragement of their parental onlookers—while he stood there waiting
in his bare feet and bewilderment. All he'd wanted to do was run
back the way he'd come, to his accustomed world. There, people
spoke a tongue not as strange to his ears as the imcomprehensible
chatter which surrounded him now, and lived a life not as frightening to his heart as that which seemed to lie before him. There, life
had a unity of its own and was complete in itself, and he belonged
to it.

The sharp report of the starter's pistol had been accompanied by the cracking of the first link between that world and himself.

At the very start of his primer school years he had panicked. He didn't know what to do or where to go. He was silent and slow in learning, reluctantly following the other primer children only because they seemed to be what was wanted of him. Tightly bunched, they sped ahead while he fell further and further behind. He could hear the roar of the crowd ahead but there were no cheers for him. Nobody likes losers. Nobody likes to be embarrassed by the spectacle of someone who shouldn't have entered the race at all. The loser is greeted with silence, averted eyes or disinterest as the crowd disperses. He may even be made fun of.

—What's the matter, Hori? Come on, lift those big feet.

He'd tried his best and had even occasionally caught up with the stragglers. But no sooner was he up with them than some obstacle tripped him and he'd fallen.

He remained way behind. All through those primer years he had been trying to catch up. He'd not entirely disliked school for he did have friends and much fun in the playground. Sometimes, when he'd negotiated a problem, mastered a new skill, he felt a satisfaction enough to make him proud of his achievement. Very occasionally, there would be a strange voice from the crowd giving him advice, or a smile among the blurred faces to give him confidence. For two brief terms of one happy year, there had been a teacher with blue-rinsed hair who would stamp his hand with stars even when he did not deserve them. Although he was kept behind for an extra year in the primers. he did not really mind. He was finding his wind.

He'd begun his standard years with much eagerness and more confidence than he'd ever had before. For one thing he was running with others who, although slow themselves, were company at least. What he'd not known was that the race itself would get harder and the rules more demanding. Already aware of his shortcomings, he was not equal to the demands. He'd begun to look over his shoulder, constantly, not for the smile or encouragement from a stranger but for the faces of Mum and Dad.

—We cannot lead from the back, Dad had told Jimmy one day.

For a long time, he'd not understood his father's words. When he did, he'd been stunned as if someone had kicked him in the stomach.

Mum and Dad. Within the confines of their own world they were not ignorant. But in the pakeha world they were already losers. They'd had no formal education, could barely write a sentence of English and their sole book was a Bible they could read only haltingly and with much difficulty. Their language was composed of broken English and broken gestures. They could never step beyond the limitations of their ignorance because it was too late for them. Their lives were already committed to the world of late night shifts, of itinerant people living itinerant lives among the black industrial areas of the towns. How could they lead him, their own son, when he already knew more about the race than they did?

Nevertheless, although they could not lead him from the front, Mum and Dad could push him from behind. They were often brutal with their pushing, angered as much as his teachers were about his apparent laziness, tardiness, carelessness, unwillingness to learn, slowness and inability to keep up with the rest of the class. If he got the strap at school, he also received a crack over the head at home. If his teacher reprimanded him for not doing his homework, he also got a growling from his mother. Once, when she'd raised her hand to him, he'd tried to lash back.

—I already know more than you do, Mum, he'd cried. You and Dad, you're dumb. You're dumb, Mum.

In her anger she'd picked up the broom and him him with it. He'd screamed with the pain and as he was screaming she'd shaken him fiercely, her face bitter.

—Bloody kid. Yes, you keep remembering that I'm dumb, you remember it. Your mother can't even spell, ay. Your father can't even do sums, ay. You damn kid, look at this house. It's a house where dumb people live, where poor people live, and I'm never going to let you forget it. Think yourself smart, ay. Think you already got a lot of brains, ay. Well, you haven't got enough yet, boy, and until you have you're going to keep on getting hidings from me. Yes, I'm dumb. Don't you be dumb like me. I won't let you, son, I won't. . . .

She'd hugged him and her anger had calmed. As she sobbed, he'd tried to comfort her. He'd begun to understand.

—I'm sorry, Mum. I'll try my best.

Never again did his mother need to treat him as violently as she had that night.

He was already doing his best. Now he began to try to do better than that. His reports had begun to improve and, by the time he reached intermediate school, they ranged from the occasional "Good" to the more usual "Needs to try harder." Once, he'd actually made an "Above Average" in English. But when the next report came along, there would be that phrase again: "James really needs to try harder." How could he possibly try harder when he was trying his hardest already! The race seemed continually to ask more of him than he could possibly give. Although he was gaining on the main bunch, he still needed someone in the crowd along the sideline to encourage him.

That someone had been Jack Simmons, the Heremaias' neighbor on the other side of the fence. After a period of uneasy peace between the two families, the relationship had settled into a friendship which flowed freely between the two houses as if no fence divided them at all. Jack Simmons had become Jimmy's teacher in the hours after school had finished for the day. He'd introduced the boy to the wider world and the wider knowledge he needed to give him the confidence to keep up in the schoolroom. He had tried to provide Jimmy with the background he'd never had, the books the boy had never read, the experiences he was afraid of, the abilities he thought he never possessed. He had encouraged the boy to enter into the pakeha world, that world so frightening to Jimmy because it was so different. With Jack Simmons leading him, Jimmy had felt a new surge of power enough to boost him past the stragglers.

But he was still far behind the main bunch.

—Don't you worry, son, Dad had encouraged him one day. You had a bad start but you're getting there, just like that horse that brought in the double last week. Nobody even thought he had a chance but he won that race all the same. People are just like horses, son. Some run a fast race, others run a slow race. You just watch. You'll be passing some of those fullas ahead of you because they'll be running out of wind!

Jimmy grinned and sneaked a look at his father beside him in the car. Who had he been trying to fool! If the other kids were running out of wind, they sure hadn't shown it. They leapt ahead and over those academic hills while he plodded slowly along like a tortoise.

It hadn't helped when he heard a teacher say:

—I just cannot imagine why the Maoris in my class are so hopeless. I am beginning to doubt if they possess any intelligence at all.

He'd felt his heart thudding with rage. Then he'd wondered if it was true. He'd asked his mother.

—You tell that teacher to stick his words up his bum, she'd sworn. You tell him to meet us on our home ground, in our own language, and we'll soon see who's intelligent and who isn't.

But the home ground was not the ground of the racetrack. Mum and Dad's world, despite its strength and beauty, was a pleasant and entertaining diversion for those who wanted it, yes, but had no place in the world of the race.

Jimmy had become suddenly aware of himself. He'd looked round and discovered that the stragglers and the ones he was now running abreast with were, like him, Maori. When he began high school, together they had formed a recognizable group to be streamed away into lower courses, to be defaulted from the race.

His mother had not wanted that to happen to her son. She insisted on enrolling Jimmy in the academic course and, when she and Dad has been asked to discuss the matter with the headmaster, she had to fight for her son in the open for the first time. On that day, when Jimmy was fourteen, she and Dad had entered through the gates of the school into the world they'd always feared. This was no time to be backward. This was no time to be shy. This was the time when she and Dad had to lead from the front.

—You know of course, Mr. Heremaia, Mrs. Heremaia, that your son is already a year older than the usual student who begins high school?

—Yes, but Jimmy's always been a late developer.

—Quite. But do you think he has developed enough to cope with the demands of the academic course?

—He can do it.

—Hmmm, that's precisely the point: *can* he? I have been looking at his academic record and, quite frankly Mr. Heremaia, Mrs. Heremaia, it is not good. Not good at all. Indeed, it falls well below the standard one usually expects of pupils enrolling for the academic course.

—We know that, but our son has to try.

—I'm afraid that trying, in these circumstances, is not enough. If one has not already got the ability, then no amount of trying will help. The academic course is extremely difficult, even for the brightest of students, and it seems to me your son is just not suited for it.

—How do you know? That record of his doesn't tell you everything about him.

—Mrs. Heremaia, it tells me all I need to know. I would urge you most seriously to consider placing your son in a course more applicable to his capabilities.

—Like where!

—Well, I gather that he is very good with his hands and the general course would appear to be his best place. I'm sure your son would be happier there, wouldn't you James? Most of your friends are there and . . .

—My son stays where he is. If I'd wanted him in the general course I would have put him there myself.

—Please, Mrs. Heremaia, there is no need to get upset. I am simply trying to tell you . . .

—Tell me what! That my son only has hands? That he hasn't any brains? How dare you. You think I don't know my own son? I'm not going to sit here and listen to you say he's no good. If you don't take him in your academic course I'll find another school that will. Education is for everyone isn't it? They can study what they like, can't they? How dare you say my son isn't good enough for your academic course.

—Mrs. Heremaia, please. You've misconstrued everything that I've said.

—But I haven't miscon-whatever-that-word-is what you think.

—But. . . .

—No buts about it. My son is enrolled in the academic course and that's where he stays whether you like it or not.

—You're being very difficult, Mrs. Heremaia. Many parents assume they know what is best for their children. Most want to believe a brilliance in their son or daughter which just simply isn't there.

—I never said Jimmy was brilliant. I'm sorry, but I want him in the academic course.

—All right, Mrs. Heremaia. As you wish. I will allow him to begin the academic course. Should you care, at any time, to change your mind about this subject, feel free to do so. I warn you that if you don't, and if James jeopardizes the progess of other pupils in his class, I myself will have no compunction about placing him in a lower form. That is fair enough isn't it? He will have to work extremely hard and I only hope that your obvious faith in him is greater than my own grave doubts about his capabilities. Unfortunately perhaps, my judgement concerning the capabilities of individual pupils has usually proved right. However, thank you for coming. Good day to you.

The interview was over. On the way home Dad had said:

—Perhaps that headmaster's right, Millie.

—Don't you ever say that! Mum had answered. And don't you ever admit it, son. None of us are going to give in so easily. None of us.

During the next four years, Jimmy had not seen much of the headmaster except on those occasions involving the whole school or when he would suddenly appear in the classroom on a round of inspection. Occasionally however, they would glimpse each other in the playground or along a corridor. At such times, the headmaster would frown before turning away. Jimmy had feared the man and was always aware that he was liable to be called to the headmaster's office at any time. His progress had indeed been painfully slow. Sometimes, when he was in absolute despair, he would actually wish the headmaster would come to touch him on the shoulder and relieve him of the struggle to catch up.

—I can't do it, Mum.

—No such word as can't, son. You must get your School Certificate, you must.

During those same four years, he also began to see less and less of his accustomed friends. One by one, as soon as they turned fifteen, they streamed away from the lower forms to become, no doubt, part of the big brown working class. Already separated from them physically, he had watched them go with increasing loneliness and envy. For them, school had been like jail. The sooner they were out of jail the better. For them the race was over.

—Mum, all my mates are leaving school.

—So?

—I'm fifteen now, Mum.

—And you want to leave too, ay? Well you're not leaving until you have School Certificate. You're not giving up so easily, I won't let you. You hear me, Jimmy? You hear me?

But not only were his friends leaving him; he, in a way, was also leaving them. His studies began to demand more and more of his time. Life itself became increasingly complicated and drew him slowly away from Mum and Dad's world. No, there was no time for diversions. Although some Maori students were able to keep a taut link between themselves and their people, his own link grew tenuous and thin. In his case, he had to commit his entire energies to the world of the race. As that commitment increased, he had become at times a stranger to his people and to himself. All for the sake of getting his School Certificate.

School Certificate. His mother was obsessed with it. For her it was the ticket allowing her son's exit from the bottom of the barrel. With School Certificate he could go anywhere. With that precious piece of paper in his hands, he could step into the life she and Dad were excluded from. The world was his once he had School Certificate.

—I tell you Mum, I just can't make it.

—Bloody kid, you'll make it all right, even if I have to drag you there with my own hands. You think I'm going to let you give up now? Not on your life, boy.

He had ended his third form year at the bottom of the class. In his fourth form year he improved his position in English, History and Geography, but was still well below average in all subjects. The next year, the spectre of School Certificate loomed ahead of him like an insurmountable hurdle. He had begun to panic. The embarrassment of not doing well, the doubts he had about his abilities and the despair of knowing he could never make it, made him balk. It seemed much easier to drop out altogether. Plead a broken leg, perhaps. Or exhaustion.

Yet he attempted School Certificate knowing from the outset he would fail. He had not expected, however, to fail so miserably.

—That's it, Mum. I've had it.

—Had it? And I've just about had enough of you too, Jimmy. I'm telling you right now you're staying at school until you get that damn piece of paper. I don't care if it takes you ten years or twenty years, you'll get School Certificate if it's the last thing you do.

She had forced him to return to the fifth form the following year. Although he still found his studies difficult, he also began to feel strange things happening to him. He began to gain a sense of relaxation and a strength he'd never possessed before. His mind had cleared, regulated his body to a steady pace and had begun to push his pace rate up higher. Steadily it rose. Steadily. Enough to boost him to a position two-thirds from the top of the class. At the end of the year, with a determined kick off the ground and a leap characterized more by desperation than ability, he attempted School Certificate again. After all these years of the race, his second wind had come to him. Although his jump was ungainly, legs and arms flailing, he made it, scraping through School Certificate with the bare minimum: 200 marks.

The roar as he landed and staggered to his feet made his heart pound with elation.

—Good on you, son. Dad had said.

—Congratulations, Jack Simmons told him.

—Thank goodness, Mum had sighed.

He had wandered in a daze for a while. Then he had started looking for a job.

—Oh no you don't, Mum said.

—But I've finished now, Mum.

—Oh no you haven't. We got to think about University Entrance now.

—I'll never make *that,* Mum.

—One hurdle is just like the next, boy. You've got the habit now. Keep it up, son. After you get your University Entrance, then you can leave school.

—But that's what you said when I was going for School Certificate, Mum.

—So what! I've changed my mind!

During those Christmas holidays, Jimmy had prepared for his sixth form year. One day, he met the headmaster in the public library.

—Heremaia, he'd said, I well remember when your parents came to see me to discuss your future at the school. Our discussion was not, as I recall, very happy. Would you convey to your parents a message from me? Would you give them my apologies and tell them that they were right and I was wrong?

—Yes sir.

—I have never been wrong before, Heremaia. However. Congratulations. And what will you be doing now?

—I'm going back to school, sir.

—Oh? Indeed?

—Mum wants me to go into the sixth form.

The headmaster had laughed.

—Well, well. I'm certainly not going to advise her again. She may prove me wrong a second time! My very best wishes to you, Heremaia.

After the holidays, he'd returned to school. He'd been the only Maori in his class and had again been the least able and least qualified of a magnificently-endowed field. However, what he did not have in natural ability, he made up with in plain mule-headed stubbornness. He clenched his teeth. All he wanted to do was keep up, keep abreast, keep going. He kept on saying to himself: If I can get this far, I can get a little further. He began to extend himself, to force himself through the year. But no amount of forcing could get him through University Entrance.

—I'm sick of failing exams, Mum.

—Kia kaha, son.

—I'm too old to go back to school. I'm eighteen now. I've done my dash.

—You're not going to get any pity from me, son. Look around you and you'll see why. This is a house of dumb people, you remember?

—Mum, what do you want from me?

She had turned on him angrily.

—Everything that you've got. And more than you've got. Nothing less. Nothing less.

He entered the sixth form for his second year. He had broken the back of the work the previous year and now he consolidated that work. Because the pace was more relaxed, he began to enjoy school for the first time in his life. More important he began to *want* to learn. There had been an English teacher, short, with glasses, who encouraged the boy to look beyond the set books and set exercises of the classroom, who opened the boy's mind to vistas formerly incomprehensible to him. Jimmy had begun to learn for the joy of learning itself. His class rating at the end of the year was a triumph, a great personal achievement. This time around, the University Entrance examination had become less fearsome. His kick from the ground had been secure, his leap an assured one, and he had cleared the hurdle with inches to spare.

—As I told you, Dad had said, some people run a fast race and some run a slow race. In the end, you get there.

His mother had sat there, her tears magnifying the gleam of triumph in her eyes.

—Who said that this was the end? she had asked.

—Oh no you don't, Mum.

—This is just the beginning, son.

—Now listen here, Mum. You said that after I'd finished getting my School Certificate you'd let me leave school.

—I know, son.

—And then you said that after I got my University Entrance, I could leave school.

—Yes, son. And so you can.

—Huh? Well, what's that gleam in your eyes for!

She had not answered him. She'd turned her head away so that he could not see her face. When she'd turned to him again, her face was tracked with tears.

—What would you like to do, son? What would you like to be?

Suddenly, he'd remembered clearing University Entrance again. He'd seen himself lifting up and over that hurdle. Right at the top of his arching jump, he'd looked back and seen where he'd come from. Then he'd looked forward and seen . . . and seen. . . .

—Oh Mum, he had sighed.

He had been pushed this far, led this far. And now? He could not stop now. He had to keep on going. He *wanted* to. He'd seen beyond the horizon. He hadn't known what was there, but he had to find out. He had to.

He'd smiled at his mother. Affectionately.

—You're cunning all right, Mum. You've lied to me and cheated me. You're not dumb at all, are you. I hope you're happy.

—Happy? If I was happy I wouldn't be crying, son. It's going to be lonely without you, that's why I cry. That's why.

He'd left home and enrolled at university in Wellington. That had been six years ago from this night. He'd been homesick and lonely and had turned for support to his relations in Wellington and the few Maori students at university. He went to Maori Club and huis, had the chance to participate more widely in the affairs of his people, but again the link had grown tenuous and thin. He could have taken Anthropology and Maori Studies but he didn't. For him, even at university, Mum and Dad's world was still peripheral to the pakeha world. He had been running for too long in the one direction to alter his course.

The pace had been killing and, although he tried his best, he failed all his units in his first year. He brooded deeply about his failure. He began to hate university but he was damned if he was going to give in to it.

In his second year at university, he gained two of his repeated units. In his third year, he saw the intelligent students graduate. He was left behind, still plodding slowly on. Would he never catch up?

He failed the same History unit three times in a row and couldn't bear to look his lecturer in the face when he met her in the street. He remembered how surprised she'd been to have a Maori, the first ever in her experience, attend her course of lectures. Her gradual disappointment in him over those three years had seemed like the growing disillusionment one senses in spectators who see a favored hurdler fail one jump after the other.

But he had kept going. He committed himself more fully to the world of the race, not only during university but also out of university. During his final years he stumbled, tripped and lunged toward his degree. One foot after the other. Round in circles. Over obstacles.

And now, that damn finish ribbon was almost in sight. Six years after having started university, he was almost there.

—Made it in one piece, Mum sighed.

She'd always complained about the way Dad drove the car. Too fast for her liking, especially when the roads were crowded like they were in Wellington.

Jimmy looked out the window of the car. Almost there. Almost at the finish. He grinned at Mum and she smiled back at him. Then she peered out at the night.

—Looks like it might rain before we get there, she said. Might ruin my fancy hairdo.

—No, it won't rain, Mum.

She dug him in the ribs.

—Come to think of it, might be just as well if it rained. Then that golliwog hair of yours might flatten out a bit, ay.

Jimmy laughed and tickled her.

—And what about Dad's shoes, ay Mum?

—Heck, that's right, she answered. Can't have the black paint running off. Your father, I don't know what's wrong with him?,

—Too late now to worry, Dad said.

Jimmy looked ahead. There, shining with lights, was the town hall like a beacon in the sky. At its floodlit entrance a crowd of people was gathering. He thought to himself: So this is what it looks like, the reception of the winners.

He felt his heart beating fast. He became impatient as Dad circled the streets round the town hall looking for a place to park the car.

—What's the rush, Dad said. You're there, aren't you?

Finally they found a park at the back of the public library—in a No Parking space. Then they joined the stream of people heading for the town hall.

—I should have worn a fur coat, Mum giggled.

—You ain't got a fur coat, Dad snorted.

—So? You could have shot some possums for me, couldn't you? she answered.

She looked at Jimmy and her eyes shone with pride.

—Never mind, she said. My son will buy me a fur coat. Ay, son.

They joined the crowd outside the town hall. Mum didn't want to go inside straight away. She was beginning to feel a little afraid. For a moment, Jimmy felt irritated with her. But then he saw others of his friends who were going to graduate tonight. From one group to the next he circulated, introducing his mother and father to them.

—How do you do, Mr. Heremaia, Mrs. Heremaia.

—How do you do.

—You must be as pleased about your son as we are about our Robert.

—Yes, we're very pleased.

Jimmy began to feel excited. As he and Mum and Dad pushed through the crowd, the happy smiling crowd, his heart began to soar. No more catching up to do! He was there, almost there.

Suddenly, Mum broke away from him with a cry. Puzzled, Jimmy watched as she rushed to the other side of the street towards a small group of people standing there. As she approached them, they began to wave furiously.

—Millie! Millie!

Dad smiled. He said to Jimmy:

—Some of your mother's relations, son. Come on.

He and Dad crossed the street. There were four people there: an old woman, a man and his wife and their young son. Mum was hugging them and kissing them in turn.

—What you fullas doing down here? she was asking. What a good surprise this is!

—Our old kuia here, the man answered pointing to the old woman, she wanted to come. She wanted to see her mokopunas. You know, Watene's kids. They live out Porirua now.

—Yeah, interrupted the wife. And this kid of ours, he wanted to come into Wellington to see the pictures tonight. Kung fu, aue! And we saw all this commotion down here so came to have a look. Is that what you're all dressed up for, Millie? You look *neat.*

Mum laughed. She motioned Jimmy closer.

—You haven't met these relations before, ay Jimmy.

She introduced him to the man and his wife and their son. Then she pressed him forward to the old woman.

—And this is one of our kuias, son. Her and your grandfather were cousins.

The old woman smiled up at him. She was waiting there, her black dress and scarf folding over her frail body. Her face was weathered with many years and her eyes were wide and luminous. She tilted her face toward Jimmy and brought her nose and lips to his. For a long moment she clung to him and Jimmy felt her tears moistening their touching faces. Then gently she broke away, wiped at her face and muttered something to Mum.

—She's giving your mother a good growling, Dad told Jimmy. Telling Mum how come she never met this mokopuna before.

Jimmy listened as Mum and the old woman talked. Then Mum looked at him and her eyes were shining with pride.

—Our kuia is very proud of you, son. I've told her about your schooling and. . . .

Mum pressed him forward again.

—This is him, she said to the old woman. And he gets his degree tonight.

The old woman nodded. She kissed Jimmy again. The man and his wife and their young son crowded round him to congratulate him. Then the old woman looked into his face and imprisoned him in her eyes.

—Aah, aah, she breated. Ka pai e tama. Ka pai. Kua u nei koe ki tena taumata o te matauranga.

Jimmy could not look away. He saw a flicker of puzzlement cross quickly over the old woman's eyes like a shadow.

—I'm sorry, he answered. I don't understand. I don't understand Maori.

The look in the old woman's eyes bruised him. He glanced across the street at the crowd gathered beneath the town hall's beacon. Then he looked at Mum and Dad and these four people standing outside the circle of the blazing lights.

These were his people, but they were not his people. This was his world, but it was not his world. He had been racing all these years. He had caught up, yes. He had won, but he had also lost.

He looked at the old woman again. She took Jimmy's hand as if to comfort him. She smiled and pressed his hand with a great and firm gentleness.

—Never mind, she whispered fiercely. *Never mind.* Congratulations anyway, boy.

A well-established writer in New Zealand, Witi Ihimaera is with the Ministry of Foreign Affairs. He was born 1944 in Gisborne and received his B.A. from Victoria University. A two-time winner of the James Wattie Award for fiction, he has published four of a projected six-book series on Maori life. Mr. Ihimaera is a member of the Te Whanau A Kai and has close links with other tribes.

"Toward the end of that summer . . .
he finally conceived what it was he needed."

The Wheel

BY JOSE V. AYALA

The toil and fulfillment of a young peasant.

THE land was Kardo's life. The land's life was his. So were its needs. There are many needs during summer. The sun stitches the earth tightly with heat. Then the waters dry up. And the land's life-giving eye becomes blind: a hole that crinkles up its edges slowly towards the center until the yielding mud becomes stone and the grass and all shallow rooted things die. The months of sweat have begun.

The sweat that ran in torrents from Kardo's body was not enough to cool the earth where it fell. Even the air was quiet and heavy in the fields. Yellow heat lit up his face and gave it life beneath a red swath of cloth wrapped around his head.

He built up parchment stalks of flint corn with short thrusts of a bolo. The double edge glinted in the sun. Dust puffed up at each blow as he moved on to the next stand of corn and to the next from one end of the field to the other.

With plow and carabao the work can be made easier. But there was no water to spare for cooling the animal's black hide. It soaked up heat like the earth. So the carabao rested beneath the shade of a bamboo grove in its wallow while Kardo shuffled under the sun among waist-high corn stalks.

The ears of corn were small this year. They get smaller every season. There was a time when each cob weighed full. Tearing the sheath open revealed tightly spaced yellow teeth. Now the ears of corn that matured barely reached the length of his palm and when the sheath was opened it mocked with the gaps of an old man's smile. Worms and green beetles scurried away from light as his hand parted another ear from its stalk. The whole field seemed to be crawling with insects.

But the corn had to be planted as it had been planted by his father and others before him.

Once more he stooped, drew his arm back and pushed down into hard earth with the blade. The blade's heel turned against a wrinkled palm. He drew out the bolo for another thrust until the circle of upturned earth surrounded the base of corn stalks.

At noon the sun stood still in the highest reach of the sky. Kardo ceased the movement of hands and began to walk home. He crossed the dry ditch that brought water and life into the fields during the season of rice.

Showing flat and watery green from a distance, the fields sloped up into more strips of corn stalks. Toward the center, where the plains began, were the brown roofs of dwellings. Beyond the clearings were more clumps of bamboo and the bell-shaped mango trees that marked the border of the town which circled away toward the sea.

On the shoulder of the hill the ground leveled off. The warm updraft of air from the valley and the plains beyond brought with it the scent of carabao dung and wood smoke. Even from a distance the strong smell of men and living things was good especially after the empty air of burning fields.

Feeling returned and sharpened dullness away from Kardo's body. The heaviness in arms and thighs lightened. Except for the bitter dryness in the mouth and the slight swelling of lips that had been clenched tightly, his tiredness eased away. A short time later he reached the shadows of green bamboos near the earthen wall that stood behind his hut.

Kardo lowered a can down the darkness of the well's mouth. Feeling the weight of water rushing into the can he pulled up the rope. Standing tall he poured the first cupful over the matted hair of his head. The water rolled down in a shining curtain, sweeping the earth from face and chest. Another cup of water and still another as the heat fell from his body with the stream, sinking into the earth from whence it came.

Lunch in the kitchen of an empty hut was salted fish and last season's rice. It was the same food he ate yesterday and the day before. Nevertheless he bolted the cold rice and the dry fish with eager handfuls. Rice had never seemed as sweet or fish as tasty. What more could a man need?

Toward the end of that summer, a long time for Kardo but insignificant to the land where two generations of his family lay buried, he finally conceived what it was he needed.

The corn had been dried under the sun and stored. The plow was ready to slice earth again, turning it over and over. But the rain clouds that gather over mountains left with the coming of evening and nights were suddenly cold with clear skies. And the heat of the earth was not enough. The thought of woman as warmth, depth, softness, troubled him while he awaited the rain. It was this that caused him to trade his corn in the village early.

She was a simple woman with long black hair parted in the middle over a broad oval face. Thick eyebrows and a flat nose accented her soft brown eyes. Her strong broad hips filled the shapeless skirt as she made sweeping movements tossing kernels of corn to chickens in the yard. Startled by his quiet staring she hid her embarrassment with a short laugh that played a dimple on her cheek. They did not speak to each other. What can he say when he does not even know her name? This was how they met the first time.

What he did not know was that she knew of him long before they met. From the neighbors, she had heard that his parents were dead and that he owned three hectares of land near the hills. She had thought of him since her last sister married. Now she knew it was her turn by the way he stared, appraising her.

Before the planting season had begun they were living together with her father's consent. There had been no priest for a church wedding. There were no priests in the hills and the city was too far away from land that was now ready for seeding.

The first night, he spoke her name in the dark quiet of the hut, and the hut was no longer dark but light. He knew then that a woman was not only warm and deep and soft, but also strong— like old rice wine.

The rice season was still young when Kardo brought Lucing to the fields. He showed her the seedling beds of rice. Green tips were already clear through water inside rectangular pools walled with banana bracts and mud. She sat on her heels and started to pick off green worms that had woven white cocoons. Between thumb and forefinger she squashed soft bodies of their green juice.

Already it has begun, she sighed. But seeing Kardo smile, drew back the quiet peace within her. And she marvelled at all the work he had accomplished alone: the green spears growing beneath her hands which he himself had sown and watered pail by pail from the well on the hill.

"The rains will soon come," Kardo said, trying to make conversation. He still found the idea of talking to a woman somewhat strange after the seasons of silence.

"I will help you build the dikes," she answered.

"This will be a good year," he said, musing at the luxury of having his thoughts answered by someone other than himself. After a while he moved on to the portion of the land as yet uncleared.

At noon she carried his meal to the fields. This, too, was a luxury. He did not have to go home for lunch. Even the work of clearing the dikes of spiny weeds seemed easy. And it also seemed to him that the afternoon was much too short. Soon the sun was setting behind the hills. When it was dark and he finally straightened his back, crickets were singing in the fields.

Two days later, clouds piled up in the evening sky. The first rain comes with the warm East wind. Drops glided down Kardo's cheeks like tears, dotting his arms with coldness. Thunder rumbled in the distant mountains and the rain became thicker. He quickened his pace. Another day of rain was needed to soften the hard soil of summer. After this he would have to plow. Already the things to be done were clear in his mind.

In the hills the wind sighed down from the mountains bringing curtains of rain. Alone in the hut Lucing heard the first drops rattling against the dry nipa-leaf shingles on the roof. The dry sharp smell of the plains came in through the kitchen window. She watched the rain falling in streams from the edge of the thatched roof straight to the ground. She was glad. For once, Kardo would not have to break his back watering the fields. Heaven would do it for him this time. But then the same nameless dread that had seized her heart when she touched the rice shoots returned. The smell of water and earth reminded her of the heavy work to be done by arms and shoulders in fixing the dikes. She had promised him and now she wondered whether she could really do it.

When Kardo came in he was smiling. He was thoroughly happy with the rain, the softening earth, and the yellow light of the kerosene lamp that flickered through the open window in the dark.

"Lucing," he called out.

"What is it, Kardo?" Lucing answered from the kitchen.

"We build the dikes tomorrow," he said, stripping off wet clothes.

"The food is ready."

Kardo stood still. The building of dikes seemed as ordinary as that to her. To him it was like rain, marking the beginning of another season. It was the first time he realized that there were some things he could not share with her. After a while he said: "Perhaps it would be better for you to stay home tomorrow instead of working the fields."

Sensing something wrong in Kardo's mind by the unsteadiness of his voice she left the kitchen to go to him. "Have I displeased you in anything?" she asked, pressing the full length of her body against his back so that their warmth was joined.

"It was nothing," Kardo said. "Just a man's thought. I would not like you to be old and bent before your time."

"That which is yours is mine," Lucing said. "I want to be with you in the fields." Her hand forced his cheek to hers. "Come now, the food is getting cold."

Kardo watched the golden light playing against Lucing's smooth arms and shoulders. Happiness rose pleasantly in him. This new kind of living held him speechless throughout summer.

The silence between them seemed to make everything all right for her. Thoughts that had bothered her were momentarily laid aside and she welcomed all the coming evenings when they would sit like this before each other, not speaking and close. Later they lay down on the mat to sleep.

Outside, the rain doubled violently, washing the dust of summer away from the thatched roof, changing the hard earth into loam. The wind seeped in through the bamboo slats on the floor bringing with it the smell of land refreshed and renewed for another season. In the fields the eye of the land filled up slowly into a pool of life-giving water, melting all the crust that had gathered, filling all the tired cracks, so that with the dawn's coming the grass seeds that had lain dormant were awakened by the abundance and began to grow.

At dawn Kardo stood bare-chested, watching a yellow streak ease darkness between land and sky. Cocks were crowing when he and Lucing sat at breakfast. They ate in silence and afterwards they walked in silence to the fields.

For the first time they worked the rice fields as man and wife. New walls were to be built where old ridges had crumbled. This was to be done before the rains set in or the water would not be contained in the fields for the rice to grow in. Kardo scraped the upper layer of sticky clay with a spade, its metal face worn smooth as a shell. Lucing was bent into an arc as she pressed into cracks in the dike the lumps that Kardo had loosened with the spade.

Heat returned to the fields as the sun rose steadily in the sky. Slowly the mud that clung to Lucing's arms and hands dried and stiffened. The effort of bending, gathering and pressing the mass of clay wrenched the softness in her. Sweat beaded her forehead and darkened the cloth against her back.

Seeing how her body trembled with fatigue Kardo said: "This is not a woman's work." The words seemed loud and harsh after the long quiet. "Here, let me be the one."

She refused. Her eyes were fixed on the ground before him. She forced a smile and continued working. Not knowing what to add to his words Kardo shrugged and moved on to the next length of dike to be fixed. Her shadow fell on the ground beside him as she followed. Throughout the hard day she thought of how her husband and the earth would always be in need until she herself became a part of the earth.

In the evening when the work was done her body seemed twice as heavy. Dried mud fell from her body as they walked home. She thought of what it was they had both done. Her weariness was overcome by comfort, knowing she had measured up to him and the land, and would not be a hindrance.

After the third night of rain the work that followed rested on Kardo's shoulders. It was now time to plow the fields three times and to harrow it each time after the plowing.

First to the East. Then towards the South. Back to the East again moved the bamboo toothed harrow until the last clod of summer was broken to pieces and all manner of weed was rooted out of the ground. The surface of the earth was cleaned and the smell of old land renewed and reopened filled the air and drew birds from the sky to a feast of worms that crawled.

The fields must be planted to rice before the blinding monsoon rainfall. The ditches that gird the fields were now full of water and the earth had drunk until it could drink no more. From dawn to dusk Kardo followed the turning earth until the heavy clay became' gray-brown mud.

Kardo let the water loose into the highest paddy. Bubbling and splashing the water fell and rushed. The silver sheet spread out and filled the first square of land. Following the shape of the earth the water sought its level as it rolled onto the next paddy and to the next. The running water flowed with force and widened over the muddy slopes, streaming on until the fields became a series of lakes within divided land.

For the last time the harrow was brought to the fields and dragged across the puddles. Deadened by water, Kardo's feet and the carabao's hoofs no longer made sucking sounds in the mud. The carabao moved forward and the mud splattered against Kardo's body. The water was warm at first. Then it got colder by the hour. Kardo's flesh became wrinkled with soaking. The last of the weeds were removed from the fields and the watered earth was now ready to plant.

By dawn-light Kardo and Lucing were still shadows in the fields. They reached the seedling beds as the sun cleared the mountains. In the gray stillness the last of the crickets sang of a summer ended.

The first touch of paddy water was cold to the bare toe. Lucing drew her shawl closer, shivered, then stepped off the dike.

Kardo plunged in without hesitation. Yielding mud made footing uneven. But he had paced the earth, morning, afternoon, evening. Now was the time for bringing life and so he spoke impatiently, "Hurry up."

Lucing nodded and moved faster through knee-deep ooze.

"Throw me one of the baskets," Kardo said, waiting before the stand of seedlings. He caught the flat-bottomed basket and set it atop the water. Gently his finger parted through the seedlings and into soft mud. More gently still, he freed a handful of green shoots and laid them on the basket. "You did well in trimming the tips," he complimented Lucing who was filling her own tray opposite him.

"It is as you wished. There are many worms," Lucing answered.

"Yes, the worms; then the weeds, then the birds. But it will be a good year. I feel it."

"I know so," Lucing said. "Two days ago I felt sick in the morning."

"It is much too soon," Kardo said. Nevertheless he flushed with excitement.

"Perhaps. But I felt it." She pressed her belly.

"Then we are in luck. The fields will be fruitful."

"Let us go, Kardo. I think we have enough."

"Ah—more than enough. Here, let me help you."

"I can manage," Lucing said, moving to the neighboring paddy.

"It cannot be soon enough for me," Kardo said to himself as he joined Lucing. Another pair of hands was more than welcome to the fields. He remembered what his father had said a long time ago: land is as rich as the number of hands that work it. As he planted the first of the seedlings he whispered, "May you be as fruitful."

Beside him Lucing worked silently. Her hands moved almost in a blur as they dipped into the basket, drew seedlings, swooped down into water, down into mud and up again for more. Soon the first paddy was filled with long rows of rice shoots.

Working side by side they went on bending beneath the morning sun. Slowly the square mirrors of water were sprinkled with green. As they rested at noonday the quiet of the fields came upon them.

In the afternoon when the sun was hottest they were in the paddies again. Lucing's waist felt broken from bending over. Stiff with dried mud the shawl stuck to her hair. The skirt she had tucked about her in the morning trailed in the water. Her hands were no longer as nimble. Water had softened them and as they pierced the mud the tender skin of fingertips began to peel off. There was also the dryness of mouth and throat. The water jug had long been emptied. What is there to drink in a field of mud?

Her husband seemed not to notice her tiredness or thirst. He had forgotten her completely. It was the merciless earth that made him forget. Only the present remained. The need for rest won. A distance away from him she drew herself up the dike. She closed her eyes. After what seemed to be a long time she opened them only to see that the sun had scarcely moved on the sky. Her body felt like one lump of mud. Forcing herself she finally gathered enough strength to stand up.

"I will prepare supper, Kardo," she explained to him as she walked away.

Kardo grunted and continued with the planting. She was a woman, he said to himself. But he could not leave off as easily. The days of planting were short and exact. If one were too early there were worms; if too late, the monsoon. So he worked in the fields until the moon rose from behind a bank of dark clouds.

When he reached the hut later in the evening he found Lucing asleep. She lay sprawled on a mat with an arm thrown across her face. In the kitchen the rice was burnt and flakes of dried mud were strewn on the floor. To Kardo, it seemed as if he and Lucing had been married for as long as the land had been cared for. He was about to wake her in anger but was overcome by pity instead upon remembering the child she carried within her. He covered her with his blanket. He did not mention the supper that had been burnt the next morning. In the days that followed she learned to work for long hours in the paddy and was no longer as tired as the first time.

Now the joy of waking up early in the morning wore off. The season of planting waned into rain. The wind that swept from mountains was cold and wet. In the fields it seemed as if the weeds had sprouted overnight between rows of rice. As fast as Kardo pulled them out the weeds grew back. It was almost as if the driving rain cultivated the grass into growing.

After the initial cold, damp sweat came. Bent over growing rice the heat of Kardo's body was a cloud of steam about him. It was hard to tell rain from sweat as water crept through his eyebrows into his eyes. He rubbed his face with muddy hands as the sweat blinded him.

Pulling the grass is easy enough when it is young. As the days passed his hands blistered. The water-soaked skin was sliced open by the sharp blades he gripped. Thorns as fine as hair stung his fingers and made them itchy. Relief came only in the evening when Lucing rubbed oil over inflamed skin. Even so, next day's work brought new discomfort with each fall of rain and growth of weeds.

At first it was annoyance that made Kardo curse the rain under his breath. Everything was damp and rot. Clothes he wore to the fields fell apart. Even the bamboo posts of the hut sprouted mushrooms from the moisture. As the days dragged on with one fall of rain after another Kardo cursed the water from the skies in anger for the fields threatened to overflow away the fruits of his labor and sweat.

Cause for hope came as the dark green stand of rice thickened with stems. Now he no longer had to weed as often for the seedlings had gained a foothold in the paddies and were several heads taller than the weeds. As slowly as the rice grew the skies cleared of clouds and the damp air from the mountains turned to the dry wind of harvest. A day came when the sky brightened with sunlight from the East. Hardly a drop of rain fell. The next morning dawned upon lakes shining in the sun. Later the fields waved in green folds with the wind.

Lucing bore the first fruit of marriage more distinctly. The front of her dress bulged out. As yet the growing child did not get in the way. Whenever the work at home was done she joined Kardo in the fields to pick worms that had been born anew with the sun. There was more time now for mending the harrow, the plow, the scythe, all the tools.

Sun-drawn, flowering stems reared up from culms and blossomed into white feathery filaments. When flower tufts had turned to soft green hulls the fields were drained. Slowly the boat-like hulls swelled up with milk. The ripening grains exuded the scent of wild flower and summer earth. Soon the fields were yellow, heavy with grain. A nameless song exulted in Kardo's blood, quickened it, and brought back the joy of being alive.

From morning until evening their two scythes flashed in the sun. Stalks fell, were caught by the hooked end of blades. A looping throw of hands tied the rice stems into sheaves which were stacked irregularly in each square of harvested paddy. Nothing was left in the fields but stubbles of straw.

The sheaves of grain were brought by carabao sled to a bare circle of earth where threshing began. Kardo whirled bundles of grain over his head in a swirl of straw dust, tearing hulls from spikes. Lucing caught the fallen hulls with a winnowing tray. She tossed the golden grain up in the air, allowing the wind to blow chaff away. The threshed sheaves were laid on the floor and again they were threshed by rubbing stalks with feet. The whole day, Kardo and Lucing moved upon straw. Together—the dust, the earth, man, woman, mingled in a seething of the harvest season until the last grain was gleaned, dried and stored in sacks.

At night with the grain safe beneath the hut, Kardo and Lucing washed off the fine dust that had hardened sweat and hair into a solid mass. By evening's light, Lucing's face was pale and her body with its distended belly looked so unexpectedly bloated that Kardo remembered her being in the last months of waiting.

"Come here," he said gently. "Let me feel the child."

She drew near and placed his palm at the soft hollow on either side of her belly.

"Well," she said, "don't you feel it moving?"

"It is kicking," Kardo laughed in surprise. "The child is kicking."

"Quite simple," she said, pushing him away as she put on her dress, "it is alive."

"Does it hurt?" he asked, seeing her wince suddenly.

"No," she gasped, the breath catching in her throat. "When it moves it takes the breath away at times."

Later when they were in the house Kardo said, "Perhaps someone should come to help when the child's time comes."

She shook her head. "I will manage. I know what to do. I have seen it often enough."

"Perhaps your mother or sister—" Kardo offered.

"My mother is too old to be walking the hills. My sisters have their children and fields to take care of. Besides, you are here."

"I do not know anything about this," Kardo protested. "I have heard it said that the first child is the hardest."

"Do not worry. My hips are wide—see? I will tell you what to do."

"As you wish," Kardo answered. Doubt of his ability to help remained to bother him.

"It is still a long time away," Lucing said. "Do not worry."

Nevertheless the worry was hidden in his mind for this problem was something new and alien to the land and to himself.

Once more the corn was wedded to the ground and the wide rim of sky, land, and the mountains beyond wavered in the heat. The sun baked the blue denim cloth to Kardo's back and across the bunched-up muscles. Steam from his body pushed out from beneath the long sleeved shirt as he bowed down again and again. The shirt smelled of hot earth, moist after the vanished rain. It was a smell reminiscent of cooling evenings and silence. Dizzy from all the bending Kardo paused a moment. But the long rows of pale green stalks with yellowing leaves mottled with violet streaks and the still untilled rows of corn that bar the earth awaited the work of his hands. The absence of Lucing from the fields and the expected coming of the child within the next day hurried him on and denied the thought of rest. Soon the incessant bending was a rhythm in which he lost himself, becoming part of the turn and fold of ground, the yellowing and burning dust that curled between toes, the heaving of breast, and the quivering heat that made the tips of all growing things wilt and shake in the stillness.

In the Philippines, Jose V. Ayala is a recognized writer and painter. He has been awarded several literary prizes and a number of his paintings hang in the National Museum. Holder of a B.S. degree in Biology and Agriculture from the University of the Philippines, Mr. Ayala has taught on the college level and is now an administrative officer for a research center.

" 'Not a betting man,' King said.
'Hate to take sucker money. Candy from kids.' "

An Early Frost

BY L.W. MICHAELSON

Smoothly written . . . enriched with mythology.

I suppose, no, I'm certain it was not the want ad itself. It was the telephone number that caught my eye:

DEAD TREES RESTORED
If Your Favorite Tree Was Killed
By The Unseasonable Frost
Phone 777-7711

I fancy myself a good amateur gambler: cards, horses, fights, you name it. And I had asked the phone company years ago for just that number to go with my avocation or my personality, if you will. Phone company officials said that such an exchange was not possible in this area. Chicago, yes, Centralia, no. In a fit of pique I called up the phone complaint department and made my pitch. No, one of those annoying voices said, after a ten-minute heel-cooling or ear-cooling delay, such a phone number could not be listed at Centralia. The newspaper ad made a mistake.

So, I called the number. Part of the attraction of the advertisement was that I was a chem and botany major in college; I knew no way of restoring dead trees myself, or I would have been up and at the task long before this. You see, I inherited this old place from my sainted Mother. Out in the backyard were her two favorite weeping willows where she used to sit reading Ronald Firbank and Jane Austen aloud to me in her shaky voice. Last September we had an early frost, killing the two willows plus an entire row of poplars that had served as a windbreak, and more practical service, to hide the garbage pail and trash bins. There were Mother's beautiful willows looking like so many sticks of bronze sculpture etched against the dark spring sky.

Mind you, I'm not overly-sentimental or a tree lover especially, but the two willows were spaced just right for hammock hanging. My mother had raised them from a pup. So, what did I have to lose? Maybe fifty bucks to some phony nursery man who alleged he could save dead trees—trees stone dead more than seven months.

I dialed this number that the phone company said was non-existent. An answering service took my message. Two days later the phone rang, and a fairly pleasant voice said: "I'm Earl King! I've come to save your trees!" There was an evangelical tone to the voice. We made an appointment for noon on the following day.

Noon, straight-up, there he was; he didn't ring the doorbell, but somehow I felt his presence. I'd just say he appeared in the vicinity of my front door, and I opened it. He was a twisted, gnarled sort; he reminded me of a timber-line spruce, bent by the wind. His skin had a funny yellow tinge to it, and his eyes, deep-set, were like floating marbles in an opaque, enameled sea. He had a little black doctor's satchel which he hugged close to his body.

All business-like, I conducted him to my twin willows. He knelt down and from the bag he took out a hypodermic syringe and filled it with some clear amber-colored fluid. The fluid looked to me somewhat like the old tincture of brownish soap we all used to shampoo our hair with. I recall I couldn't get close enough to smell the mixture, although I stood as close as I could when he stuck his needle near the base of the trees.

It, the operation, was all over in seconds. The syringe and amber fluid bottle were popped back into his satchel. "Fifty dollars down and fifty later, when your trees leaf out," he said.

I hesitated. "Ah . . . well," I stammered. "Somewhat reasonable, but how do I know this shot in my trees' fanny will work?"

"Good question," Earl King said. "Give me a postdated check, three weeks from now."

"Got yourself a deal," I said. "Betcha another clean fifty, nothing happens."

"Not a betting man," King said. "Hate to take sucker money. Candy from kids."

"Okay," I said. But I made the check out for four weeks ahead. Mr. King did not glance at the check but jammed it in his shirt pocket. "Be back someday soon," he said, and then he went quickly though my house and out to his car, a funny-looking foreign sedan. An odd car for a tree man, I thought as he sped away. No place to stow dead limbs and such.

In three weeks we were launched into our hot summer. The "we" is myself and my Mother's dog, Tooky, an old white Samoyed. Tooky often stretched out under the willows in the summer, and Mother would scratch his ears and they would both nap away the long afternoons. Much to my amazement, in the stated time the willows leafed out. I hunted up the want ad then. How dumb of me, I thought, not to have him give a shot to the poplar trees while he was here. But then, alas, the bill would have been more, and there might have been more risk with the poplars, which were dead as dead can be. I called 777-7711 anyway. Nothing. Nothing, but a recording from the phone company: "The number you have dialed is not listed. Please ask information for the correct . . . ." I slammed the receiver down.

Well, to hell with it all, I thought. I called up my bank and cancelled the check. Maybe that would bring Mr. King around. The willows, meanwhile, blossomed out, greened out beautifully. In fact, incredibly! Weeping willows have no blossoms, as far as I know, and my trees were now covered with tiny red blossoms, that gave off a rather strong, but delightful fragrance. I was enchanted. I called back the bank to uncancel my check. "What was the number of that check?" the teller asked. I looked up my stub. "Ah . . . 777," I said. "And then, 7711." Well, I had made a mistake the teller said. My checking numbers were in the zero, zero-twelve series. But anyway, no post-dated checks for fifty dollars had been cashed on my account. So, I forgot about it all.

I forgot about the trees, too, pretty much. I had to cut down a good many branches to put up my hammock. The darn trees were unusually lush. More like jungle growth than regular willow greenery. And there were strange-looking bugs flying around underneath the two, and I spotted a green gecko lizard zipping off into the grass, as I lay in my hammock. All in all, the place didn't seem too pleasant a place to have a hammock anymore. But tradition is tradition. And I managed to lie there now and then. It seemed uncommonly hot under all those sheltering limbs now: humid, jungly. Not like a nice, orderly, weeping willow in a town there 5,000 feet above sea level. But Tooky seemed to like to stay out there.

And it was Tooky's strange death that made me start this search. I found Tooky, who was old, it is true, and who did have asthma, stone dead under the willows, her shaggy body covered with yellowish pollen from these red flowers. To be sure, I took Tooky to a vet and in my presence he began an autopsy. "Lungs pretty good for an old dog," the vet said. "I dunno why she died. Stroke maybe."

"Cut up the head," I said. "But I'll come back tomorrow." I couldn't stand to see old Tooky butchered this way.

"A complete autopsy will cost around one hundred," the vet said.

"Worth it," I said, and I wrote out a check and I almost put down the check number as 777-7711, but then I stopped myself.

Two days later the vet called. "I'm returning all but twenty dollars of your money. I don't know why the dog died. It just died. These things happen with older dogs."

"Well, I'm damned!" I said. And I went out then and lay down in the hammock with a novel by Firbank, *The Flower beneath the Foot,* and a big glass of iced-coffee. This last so I wouldn't go to sleep. In twenty minutes or so there were all these tiny flowers drifting down on top of my hammock, and I was starting to be covered with a whitish, yellowish pollen, and I felt smothered: something like an asthma attack. And I got up in a hurry and took some of the pollen and a tiny blossom or two and put them under my own microscope, an instrument salvaged from my college days, and looked at these strange little spores and anthers. Never saw or heard of them in any botany text I had.

What to do? I'll get the son-of-a-bitch, I said. And I placed a want-ad in the local paper: "$500 reward for someone who can save my trees—killed by the Frost." No takers. Except a salesman from a nursery came out and tried to sell me an entire new landscape job.

So, I forgot about it all. Stayed out of my backyard entirely. Went to the horse races, played poker, came out way ahead, money-wise. Then I closed up the house, and moved to an apartment where I stayed until fall. The weather in Centralia then was unusually mild: Indian summer. But I did read in the papers how an "unseasonable frost" had killed all the trees in the small Colorado town of Big Junction. I said, *hmmm* to myself, and hopped in my car and drove some 400 miles to the town and holed up in a motel. Nothing much happened the first week; I mean, no interesting want ads in the local paper. So I drove to a larger town with a shopping center and bought a red wig, a false moustache, and heavy dark sun-glasses.

Then I came back to Big Junction and, under an assumed name, rented a large frame house that had a backyard full of frost-damaged trees, subscribed to the local paper, and sat back to wait. I bought a white dog, too. This time a year-old Spitz.

About seven days later, there was the want-ad!

> Call Erl King
> If Your Trees Were
> Damaged by Frost
> 777-7711

I called the number, gave my message to the answering service and sat down at my front door to wait. Nothing happened. *Hmmm,* I said. I went to the local hardware store and bought a heavy spade and a 16-gauge shot-gun. And sat down again by my front door. Two days after this, about noon, I got a tingly feeling, and flung the door open. There he was.

"I'm Earl King, the tree man," he said. "Sorry about the delay. Got tied up with some kids."

"How do you spell your first name," I asked. "E-r-l, or E-a-r-l?" "Ah . . . ah . . . a misprint in the paper. But it's an old German name."

"From Konig?" I asked.

He gave me a hell of a penetrating look with those funny marble eyes. "How about your trees," he said in brisk, business-like tones.

"Trees? Right this way," I came back. I led him through the house to the backyard. My new white Spitz growled at him en route. "This weeping willow and those two poplars need fixing," I said.

When he bent down to open up his satchel, I struck him with the heavy spade that I had kept handy. Erl King, or whoever he was, slumped over without a sound. I was about to bash him another blow on the side of the head for good luck, but then I really had no evidence about Tooky's death. In fact, I wondered on just what impulse I had hit him at all. Perhaps I could take over his magic tree formula and make a bundle—but I didn't really need money that badly.

Poor man, I thought then. He never even tried to cash my fifty buck check. Well, what was done was done. Luckily, the house was isolated from neighbors and the backyard enclosed by a high fence; they'd find him next spring, if at all. I took his satchel, checking it first for the syringe and the amber fluid, jumped into my already-packed car and left town at a good clip. I drove to Centralia, put the Spitz in a kennel, and then took a plane for Chicago and the small university where I got my biology degree.

Some two days later I was in the school lab with my old prof of bio-chemistry, Dr. Klein. My question was: "What is this stuff? It brings trees back to life." I added: "we can make a million!"

Working together, we ran the liquid through a detailed chemical analysis. This took the better part of a day, and at the end of that time, Dr. Klein threw up his hands. "I give up! You know this liquid looks and acts like snake-venom of some kind. And guess what?"

"What?"

"I've never seen the like before. An alkaloid base, some high density protein molecules, but . . . but . . ."

"Let's shoot some of the stuff in an old tree?"

"Well, maybe later," Dr. Klein said. "Right now let's shoot some in a white lab mouse."

Poor mousey was dead in thirty-nine seconds by a stop-watch.

"Well, now what?" Klein asked. "No dead trees around Chicago right now—that I know of."

"Get a two-day leave of absence from this jerk place and come out, at my expense, and look at my willow trees."

The three days I was in Chicago I, of course, bought all the Colorado newspapers I could lay hands on. No mention of any dead or injured found in a yard in Big Junction. Luckily I had rented the old house there under a phony name. No way they could trace the real me; I mean, the Big Junction police would have a problem or two. I wasn't so sure about Mr. King.

En route back to Centralia, I told Dr. Klein the whole bit. Shortly after we arrived, I went to the boarding kennel to pick up my Spitz and left the professor snooping around my yard. He kept busy hacking away at the jungle-like branches and creepers, looking at the leaves and blossoms under my microscope. The damn trees meanwhile had usurped almost my entire backyard! Finally, we found the dead stumps of the old willows.

"This monstrosity you have here," Dr. Klein said then, "is a *new* tree, not a rebirth. This tree . . . ah . . . it's new to me. You sure your tree man didn't plant a few seeds while he was wielding the syringe?"

"What seeds could sprout into a tree in a few weeks?"

"Maybe he cast a spell, raised his arms in a benediction, whispered a magic incantation."

"Absurd! He bent down and stuck a needle in the trunks, and that's all."

"This monster here is something like the Banyan tree of India or maybe the peepul tree: all roots and creepers. If I don't miss my guess there's a snake skulking around its roots. Your dog, Booky? Tooky? It was bitten is my guess. A krait maybe?"

"Surely the vet could diagnose snake-bite?"

"Well, he'd know a rattler bite, being in Colorado. But a member of the *elapid* family—I don't know."

"Hah! An elaborate plan for some strange man to kill poor little me. Expensive, time-consuming, stupid! Why didn't he just shoot me?"

"He could have very well stabbed you with his needle. No noise. You'd be dead in two minutes. No one would know why or how."

"Or maybe I'd sprout into a Banyan tree? Absurd!"

"Ah . . . any bad gambling debts? I remember at college you were quite the one to . . . ah . . . ."

"Nary a one! I'm clean as a whistle, welch-wise."

"What was the man's name again?"

"Earl King."

"*Das Erl Konig!* Ever hear of Schubert's song?"

"Oh, come on now, prof! Hear it? Why I can even sing it after a fashion. My mother's favorite."

At this, Dr. Klein looked at me sadly.

"All right!" I said with some irritation. "So, he's das Erl Konig. And he's 7,000 miles or more from his home base in Germany. And why me? Why me in this hunky mountain town in Colorado? And how do you figure I could bash him on the head with a shovel and not get hurt back, pronto?"

"Really doesn't add up very well," said Dr. Klein. "Just why did you hit him? We don't know why your dog Cooky or Hooky died."

"An impulse," I said. Klein sighed heavily at this. "Okay!" I said, "a *childish impulse!* But why does all this guff happen to me?"

"Job asked the same thing. Meanwhile, buy a mongoose; keep a shot-gun handy. Stay out of your backyard."

"Out of the yard!" I exploded. "Out of this damn town!"

"Well," Klein said then, "I wouldn't let any old Erlking push me around. He's supposed to annoy children, *only,* anyway. By the by, did you *ever* marry?"

"Well, up to now, I've been very comfortable here with my Mother and my . . . ah . . . habits," I answered. I was about to add, *you nosey old coot,* but I thought better of it.

I sent Dr. Klein back to Chicago the next day. What a sarcastic bastard, he was! I decided to put the old home up for sale, live in it until it was sold, and then clear out to New Zealand or some far off place. No sense letting a German mythological character get the best of me. I didn't get a mongoose, of course, but I kept my 16-gauge shotgun handy. And I put out a pan of milk; poisoned, of course, and I kept my doggy inside.

Really, I didn't want to stay in the old house, but it was more convenient to do so; potential buyers dropped in at all hours, and it was best that I be on hand instead of some indifferent real-estate agent. So I stayed on. One time, early in the morning, I woke up with a strange tingling sensation. I ran to the bedroom window that looked out on the backyard. In the dim light, I swear, I saw my mother resting in the hammock, scratching old Tooky's ears. I tried to call out to her, but I seemed paralyzed.

After that, I thought I would lose my mind. So I started to drink heavily. I had plenty of time, too, to reflect about Mother, about my past. About Dr. Klein's question, damn him; *why didn't I ever marry?* Why the hell didn't I? Too comfortable being a bachelor. Don't get me wrong; I had girl friends. But they meant trouble, responsibility. I got rid of them fairly quickly. None of them ever matched Mother for understanding, for good cooking, for . . . for sympathy. So I didn't grow up exactly; I mean, mature. But really nobody's damn business. Mother left me considerable money, and so . . . And so?

But the Erlking comes for all children—if they remain children too long, that is. I read up on the old German folk-tale. This evil spirit was meant to frighten *kinder* when they'd been bad. But he supposedly carried off quite a few also . . . to . . . to Erl King land, I guess. I read about the Banyan tree, also. *Ficus Bengalensis.* Sometimes the tree would grow and grow and whole villages could settle under the branches. But there were disturbing folk tales about dark spirits inhabiting the Banyan; one could easily imagine the snake-like roots reaching out at night to crush a victim. Truly, not a pleasant tree to have in one's backyard; I think it hurt the sale of the house, too. Potential buyers would be pleased about the house until I conducted them to the yard, and then there would be silence and a hasty departure.

But I kept to my post. Perhaps there would be an early frost and it would kill every damn thing in the yard: snakes, roots, lizards, Lord knows what. But then this thing about my dreams. The dreams, at least, defeated me. I'm not a coward exactly. I didn't quite dare lie out on the hammock underneath the willows, but on a garden lounge chair fairly nearby.

I decided the last night, my last night, in the real world, to sleep out in the yard all night. I had my shotgun and a quart of gin. Mother drank gin; tradition is tradition. I drank myself into a stupor, and fell asleep. I dreamt that a very large cobra was twining about the willow trees, the Banyan tree. And then, in this last dream of mine I felt—no, I knew! I knew that I was the tree, a young tree, a child of a tree. I kept calling for my mother, and then . . . and then . . . the cobra spread its hood, an enormous hood that blotted out the sky, and struck out at me. I remember I got up from the lounge chair screaming, "Quick! Mother! An antidote!"

But there was no one there. Nothing. I wrote Dr. Klein right after the nightmare. A rambling incoherent letter. Something about the Erl King. I got one back, almost immediately:

Dear Tooky: I'm more disturbed about you than any shrubbery in your backyard. Due to smog, etc., the polar caps are melting and our climate is changing. Tropical plants will be common in your area. But you, Phocian, why don't you get married and settle down? Quit brooding about your Mother and the past. The Banyan tree is in your mind, *n'est-ce pas?* Just for kicks, see a headshrinker?

Horse manure to you, old buddy, I thought. But then, Dr. Klein with his twisted frame, and funny eyes—eyes twisted from peering into microscopes, reminded me of Earl King. I sent him an air mail letter right back which said: "I hate you, Earl King Klein."

So? So, I took his advice and went into group therapy. Damn, if somehow, Dr. Klein, in a sense, had me committed. The doctor and the rest, they laugh at me. But I know there was an Erl King, and he'll come for me someday. Although I do feel somewhat safer here in the rest home with the drugs and all. But he'll come for me—I know it, I know it! Just the other day there was an early frost.

If only Tooky were here to bite someone for me. If only my mother . . . she . . .

L.W. Michaelson, a native of Colorado, devotes himself to writing and teaching. He received his PhD from the University of Denver. His short stories appear in several magazines.

"Get yourself dried off, especially behind
the ears. Roll into bed and pull up the covers and
dream us up another nightmare."

The Prevaricator

BY CARLOS BAKER

This story may bring to mind the boy who cried "Wolf!"

HIS watch said ten past ten when the Sea Sled whipped into sight
around the wind-lashed corner of East Point and went roaring past
the Spindle. Its blunt nose was better than a yard out of water, and
behind it the powerful propellers hurled a thick white feather of
spray high into the air. From where he stood on the wide veranda,
he could see the hull slapping every second ground swell with
what he knew must sound like pistol shots.

He could not hear the sound because of the nearer one that the
wind was making, howling around the corners of the house. The
flag on the pole beside the Coast Guard Station streamed out
straight. On the rocky beach big combers still clawed at the
pebbles and over all the visible sea were heaving blankets of foam
and seaweed. Tons of white water were still pouring and sloshing
over the top of the red granite rock they called Elephant's Back.
Even the air was thick with salt spume, and shreds of hurrying

cloud, the last remnants of the first big storm of the season, blew like battle smoke all across the proscenium arch of sky between East Point and South Point.

He raised the binoculars for a closer look at the plunging Sea Sled. Its course was due south through the deep water just beyond Beach and Rock Islands, and he picked them up as they cleared the highest bulk of Beach Island, two heads crouched in the cockpit close together.

Then a strange thing happened. The whole craft seemed to gather itself like a hooked and angry swordfish, leaping clear of the water almost the way those racing boats in the Everglades take a low hurdle. For a second or two it lurched wildly, veering out to sea, but whoever was steering yanked her back on course, the plume of spray dropped down, and for another few seconds she bobbled like a broken toy in the scramble of the waves. Then he saw the nose coming up and around, the tail plume feathering aloft once more, and in astonishment he lowered the binoculars to watch that crazy pair of idiots ramming her right across the dangerous water of the shoals inside Rock Island, heading like an arrow for the Coast Guard cove.

He slide the glasses into the leather pouch beside the front door, vaulted the veranda railing to the lawn, splashed through the mud puddles in the road, and ran for the cove, the tough sea grass whipping against his bare legs and feet. Up in the window of the Coast Guard watchtower he could see Red Horsfield's mop of hair, and he cupped his hands and yelled, pointing at the sled. Red stuck out his head, then his shoulders and half his torso, his mouth opening in a black O as he yelled something in reply, but the wind ripped and scattered whatever it was he was saying.

Griff could hear the engine now, plosive as a distant drumbeat. From the water's edge where he stood the oncoming bow looked enormous. Two hundred yards offshore the steersman swerved to clear the rocking covey of the Coast Guardsmen's skiffs and dories, and now he could see both faces—wind-reddened blobs under sailor hats pulled down around their ears. He waited for them to shut off power and drift in the rest of the way, but there was no break in the pounding roar and in amazement Griff leaped aside out of their path. At the last possible moment the driver cut the engine, the plume slapped down, and the whole forward part of the sled crunched heavily on the egg-sized stones of the beach.

One of the men was over the side like a monkey. His khaki pants and the heavy shawl-collared navy blue sweater were soaked and he wore red and white deck shoes. He had pulled off the sailor hat and was stuffing it into his hip pocket. The breakers curled around his knees as he waded ashore and squatted down beside the bow. "Look at that," he said. "For Christ's sakes will you look at that?"

Just aft of the prow was a gaping hole in the sled bottom. Daylight showed through. Torn splinters of wood hung dripping around the edges.

"By God, look at that," the short man said again.

The man at the wheel was easing one long leg stiffly over the gunwale. With evident distaste, he swung down into the water and moved slowly towards where Griff was standing, throwing him a kind of ironic salute. "Morning, Cap," he said in a booming bass. "Can't you do something to warm up this Maine water?"

Griff grinned back at him. "It'll warm up in August," he said.

"So I've heard tell," the limping man said, "and do in part believe. But it sure isn't warm in July."

His yellow oilskin parka dripped with moisture and Griff saw that there was a slash of blood on his left cheek. He sat down stiffly on the stones and began to rub one of his knees tenderly.

"The thing I can't figure out," he said, partly to Griff and partly to the other man, "is *what* we hit." He fixed Griff with a blue-eyed stare. "What *did* we hit, Cap? Can you tell me that?" He waved his unoccupied hand vaguely seaward.

"Nothing out there but water," Griff said. Anton Staples, the Coast Guard captain, was picking his way over the wall of kelp that the storm had washed up. "Deep water, too. The chart shows fifteen fathoms."

"Except for that goddam rock in the middle of it," the short man said. He was still hunkered down under the bow, fingering the jagged splinters.

"No rocks there," Griff said quietly. "Here's the captain. You can ask the captain."

Anton came up puffing, his cap askew as always, each of his chins separately quivering. "Something wrong, boys?" he said in his high-pitched voice.

The man under the bow spoke again. "Nothing but half the bottom tore out."

"How come you come in full throttle?" asked Anton.

"Keep the nose up," the little man said shortly. He found a blue rag in the pocket of his sweater and mopped his face with it. "Bow tore out, you got to keep the nose up or else drown."

Anton chewed his morning cud slowly. His small observant eyes swept the craft. "Likely it was them ground swells," he said. "You come down from Portland?"

"Boothbay," the older man said.

"You hit a lot of ground swells between Boothbay and here," Anton said. "One plank loosens up and you hit a ground swell just so and you're a goner. Ain't that right, Swiv?"

Griff winced at the old nickname, his bugbear since childhood. Swiv or Swiveon, short for the Swivel-Tongued One, invented ten years ago by his professor-uncle, boiled down to Swiveon by his mother, who said it was a very poetic name, and cut to Swiv by his father, who still sometimes used it to get his goat. It did, too, because it stayed in his mind as the badge of that time, the really bad time, when he was fighting to be believed, when they would all look askance and grin quizzically at each other the minute he opened his mouth to tell them about anything that had happened to him. "The ring-tailed roarer," the professor-uncle said. "The supreme prevaricator. The vendor of Bologna."

Griff would leap up in a rage and go storming out of the house because they would not believe the things he wanted to tell them. Even the true stories that he told with such care to replace the kid stories that he had only half-believed himself. How long would it take for them to forget all that and bury the hated nickname for all time?

He cleared his throat. "It's rough enough out there today," he said to Captain Staples. "Coming from Boothbay all that pounding could have loosened the boards."

The tall man arose from the stones and limped over to shake hands with Anton. "Name's Williamson," he said in the booming bass voice. "That's Pete Mapes in the wet britches."

"Cap'm Staples," Anton said with dignity. "This here's Swiv Axton. Like he says, nothing out there past the island but a lot of rough water."

Pete Mapes stood like a pint-sized athlete, blunt red hands on his hips, doubt in his pale eyes. "Could be a dory tore loose from somewheres," he said.

Anton placed a large right hand on his whitish shirtfront to hold the black service tie in place and leaned forward to spit. "Could be the *Lucy Tanya*," he said with a lopsided grin. He turned towards the watchtower where Red Horsfield still leaned from the window. "Hey, Red," he called. "You want to take that glass and glom her over out there where they say they hit something. Could be they hit some floating objick. See what you can see."

The bronze snout of the telescope appeared in the window, moving slowly back and forth. Then it withdrew and the red head replaced it. "Too rough yet," Horsfield called. "All riled up. Can't make out nothing."

"It's a nothing that is something," Williamson boomed. "Hoisted us clean out. You could hear it smack."

Anton pursed his lips as if he were going to spit. "We got a shorthanded crew here right now," he said, "or we'd take a little run out there and have a look-see. Could be driftwood. Could be a log come down the Saco."

"Could be Moby Dick the white whale," said Williamson.

"Tell you what," Anton said. "I'll get the cutter on the phone, see'f they'll take a run down here. Might be a powerboat capsized and bottom-up. That would do it. Something like that counts as a mare-time hazard. You boys come on in, get warmed up. Come on, Swiv, time for a coffee break."

"Griff," the boy muttered, but a gust of wind blew out the word like a match flame.

Eating lunch alone in the Axton kitchen he wondered again for the thousand and first time how long it took to get rid of a liar's reputation. For years now it had stuck with him like a cockleburr, made him turn laconic, made him choose every word with care, never uttering a sentence that was anything but the truth. And nobody seemed to notice.

All around him every day there were people talking, yarning, telling anecdotes that they refurbished to make them sound better, to dramatize them, stories that only grazed the truth if they came anywhere near it. Red Horsfield for one, telling how he had lied—yes, lied—about his age and got into the army at fifteen. He said it was his seventeenth birthday when they went in on Casablanca, and he could go on for an hour or more any time about the back streets and alleys and Arabian babes in every North African city from Casablanca to Bizerte. Lies, most of them. Or take Anton Staples for another, sagged back in the captain's rocker, chewing his quid, as swivel-tongued and smooth-talking as they came, and nobody contradicted him or seemed to question anything he said.

But let Griff Axton get out the first sentence of a truth he knew and the old doubting-Thomas look began to show on all the faces—even Red's, even Anton's—and the room would fall so quiet that his voice would drop and trail off and he would begin clearing his throat with embarrassment in the atmosphere of disbelief and after a decent interval Anton would shift his quid into one cheek and start again, "Swiv, I ever tell you about the feller that—"

Griff stopped chewing and tossed the sandwich aside with distaste. The name was a habit by now, and habits dissolved slowly. There was nothing to do but call them on it each time, saying *Griff* firmly as soon as they said *Swiv,* just as he had done with Anton that morning. He scraped the rest of the lunch off the plate into the garbage pail, slammed down the lid, found the old red swimming trunks and a pair of battered sneakers, and went down to bail out his skiff.

The wind had dropped now and the sea was flat, though the air remained as sticky as ever. The station flag hung limp, a tri-colored splash against the monochrome of hazy blue. In the wide inlet directly in front of the house, the skiff pulled placidly at its rope. He saw that the storm had left it half full of water and weed.

Downshore in the station cove the Sea Sled still lay where they had slammed it full throttle through the morning breakers, but the ebbing tide had left it high and dry. For the first couple of hours, all the curious had come from miles around to marvel at the ripped floorboards, theorizing about the cause. In the end they had fallen silent, gazed speculatively out to sea, and departed. Mapes and Williamson had gone off, too—ignominiously enough—on the noon bus to Portland. Everything was silent now, like an empty room.

He picked up an old jam tin from the jetsam on the shore and waded out to his skiff. The cold water bit at his ankles. Up in the station watchtower he could see Poquelin's bald head, standing the watch from noon to four because they were shorthanded now, with Sikes's ruptured appendix and Hank Simons off on liberty. Later, he knew, the captain would puff his way up the stairs to relieve Poquelin while he cooked supper. Red Horsfield would come yawning out of his dormitory sack to sniff the steam of the kettles on the stove, insult Poquelin's cooking, eat it swiftly and noisily, pick his teeth while he listened to the six o'clock newscast, go outside to haul down and stow the station flag, and get squared away for the eight-to-midnight watch in the tower.

It occurred to him to beach the skiff and dump the water all at once. But it was pleasant to stand out there beside it, watching it buoy up slowly as he bailed it out, canful by canful. When it was nearly empty he got in and sat in the stern. The captive water gurgled cool around his feet as he bailed steadily—*slup, slosh, slup, slosh*—so absorbed in the rhythm that he barely heard his name being called.

"Swiv. Swiv Axton." It was Red Horsfield's voice from the shore. He did not break the rhythm of his bailing or turn his head.

"Hey, Griff."

So it had worked this time. He turned and waved with the bailing can. Red stood near the water's edge, the white gob's hat on the back of his flaming mop of hair.

"It's your bedtime," Griff said. "You're supposed to be in the sack."

"Couldn't get to sleep," Horsfield said. "Too muggy, like a darned oven up there. Kep' thinking about that Sea Sled. They swore up and down they hit something big. Short man says it was huge."

"What did he think it was?"

"Going too fast to tell," Horsfield said. "Says they leap-frogged. Says the darn sled took off in the air for twenty or thirty feet. Says if they'd have held out their arms they'd be airborne yet."

There was a tall tale for you, and Red Horsfield telling it like gospel truth. Griff slipped the painter, unshipped the oars, and pulled ashore.

"Let's go on out there and check the spot," he said.

"Who's rowing, Swiv, you or me?" asked Red.

"Me. And the name is *Griff*."

"Okay, let me just slip off my Sunday shoes." He left them with his socks at the edge of the sea grass and came limping back over the stones. "I swear I don't know which hurts the worst, barefoot or Sunday shoes," he said, climbing in. He began to roll up the legs of his pants. "You row out and I'll row back," he said, and then, like an afterthought, "Griff."

Griff rowed steadily and expertly along the route they always took, following the edge of the wide trench that made in past the southern tip of Beach Island like a submarine avenue. The gut, they called it locally. Ordinarily you could read the dimensions of the trench by the bobbling line of lobster buoys that led in a long curve to the gap between Beach and Rock Islands. But not today. The storm had ripped everything loose, tossed the buoys and even some of the traps ashore. Or almost all. He grazed one of the buoys with an oar going past. It was painted green and white to show that it belonged to Harry Phillips, the English-born lobster man.

"Where's your folks, Swiv?" asked Red.

Griff ignored the question, rowing rhythmically.

"I ain't seen 'em around today, have I?"

"Gone up to Seal Harbor," Griff said shortly. In the thick humidity he was beginning to sweat. "Back tomorrow night."

As they neared the island, all the gulls and terns leaped aloft, mewing and bleating, afraid you would come ashore and step on the eggs they had laid on the dry patches of seaweed among the stones. Griff pulled on past to where the ground swells, huge and slow, swept majestically under the skiff. Over Red's shoulders he could see the line of cottages along the shore—Phillips, Fletcher, Axton, then the break where the Coast Guard property began, then the red-roofed, white-painted bulk of the station itself. He took a rough bearing on his own front porch, the watchtower, and the southern tip of the island, and then paused, letting the oars trail in the water.

"Just about here," he said.

"I'd a said they was a little more south," Horsfield said.

"We'll look around," Griff said, beginning to row again.

Red shaded his eyes with both hands, peering out on either side. "Course we don't stand no chance," he said. "Whatever they hit, if they hit a log or even a dory, we ain't going to find it."

"The wind dropped down fast once it dropped," Griff said. "Anything really big couldn't have drifted far."

"No harm looking," said Red, yawning.

But they zigzagged all over the area for an hour without finding anything except acres of floating seaweed that the storm had torn from the bottom.

"Here now," said Horsfield at last. "Let me row her back. Time we get back in, supper'll be on the table."

Griff changed seats, stretching his legs in the stern, letting his hands trail in the cold water. The west-running sun was in his eyes now, and he turned his head, watching the glitter it threw on the calm surface down by South Point. It was just there that he had seen the swimming deer, late one July morning six or seven years ago, the lifted antlers black as tar in the midst of all that shimmer. That was soon after he had taken the tumble on the rocks and broken his wrist. He was still wearing the cast and standing on the high white granite rock beside the cove where Harry Phillips kept his old powerboat. Harry was transferring the morning's catch into the floating lobster car.

Griff had watched the deer for a full minute before he opened his mouth. It was a deer all right. It was swimming steadily out to sea. Dogs must have scared it in the woods and chased it and it had taken to the water to get away. Now it would drown.

"Hey, Harry," Griff yelled when he was sure of what it was. "There's a deer out there."

Harry Phillips did not pause in his work. "Out where?" he said.

"Way off South Point," Griff said. "I can see the horns. It's swimming out to sea."

"Swiv, boy, you look again," said Harry, grinning. "Likely you might change your mind. You'll see it's an old tree and them horns would be the branches."

"No, Harry," Griff yelled. "Honest to God, Harry. It's moving. I can see it swimming."

Deliberately as always, Harry closed the top of the lobster car, turned the wooden pivot that locked it shut, wiped his hands on a piece of engine waste, found the sack of Bull Durham, rolled and lighted a cigarette, and looked up to where Griff stood on the rock high above his head.

"Twelve-point buck, I'll bet," he said. "Tell me another, Swiv, old boy. I ain't heard a good one today."

High on his granite perch, Griff almost danced with frustration. It was a full four minutes before Harry would even stop grinning, his broad red face creased with seagoing wrinkles. He smoked the cigarette hungrily until it was a butt, flipped it overside, rinsed his hands in cove water, turned down the tops of his rubber boots, and at last came lumberingly up the rock to where Griff stood. He stood squinting towards the shining waters off the Point.

"Now just where was it you seen that buck?"

Griff pointed with the plaster cast, unable to speak.

"Swimming, you said. Horns sticking up."

"Yes. Yes."

"Now, Swiv boy," said Harry. "With the best will in the world I tell you I got pretty good eyes but I don't see one damn thing."

Griff peered uncertainly through the glimmer, his heart like a stone sinking in a puddle. In all that vast stretch of water there was nothing in sight. His eyes flushed hot. "You waited too long," he cried. "Now it's gone and drowned. We could have got out there and brought him back. Now it's too late."

Harry looked uncomfortable. "Maybe so, son," he said kindly. "And *if* so, we could have brought him right back here and turned him loose. Or we could have hit him over the head and had us a nice mess of venison. *If* we could have started the motor and cast off and got out there in time. Trouble is, we couldn't. Not under twenty minutes, and it ain't but ten since you said you seen him first." Slowly, his big shoulders bent, boots clomping, Harry lifted his gear and began climbing the gravel path up the bank to his house.

"Back the same day," Red Horsfield said. "You feel all right? You ain't said a thing for ten minutes."

"Sure," said Griff distantly. "Just hungry is all."

"You got some supper at the house?"

"She left enough to feed an army."

Red shipped the oars and stretched his arms. His freckled forehead was running with sweat. "You want to tie up out there or leave her in here? Tide's starting to come."

"I guess I'll pull her up to the grass."

"Grab aholt, then," Horsfield said. "Old Cokey's putting my grub on the table right this minute."

They dragged the skiff to the edge of the sea grass. Red found his shoes but did not stop to put them on. "See you later, Swiv," he said, hurrying up the path.

"So long," Griff said absently. He was still thinking about Harry Phillips and the swimming buck.

Something woke him in the humid darkness of the bedroom and he rose on one elbow to read the luminous dial of his watch. Ten forty-five. Stifling still and quiet. Twelve hours ago the wind had been tearing at the shingles like a crazed animal. Now no breath of air so much as stirred the curtains and except for a sound like a far-off sigh, you would not even know that the sea was there.

He rolled free of the sticky-feeling sheet and crossed to the window. In the faint moonlight, rocks and water made a pattern in black and silver. For a moment he stood hesitant in the semi-dark by the window. Then he found the faded swim trunks on the chair, pulled them on, and let himself out of the front door. In less than a minute he was standing beside the high-and-dry skiff, feeling the cool breath of the risen ocean.

He waded in and plunged quickly, making for the flat-topped rock at the far edge of the inlet, just where the gut swung past. He lifted himself clear and sat down dripping. A high layer of cloud half obscured the moon, and he could see the faint light in the watchtower. Red Horsfield would be sprawled in the wooden chair, reading a copy of *Field and Stream,* getting up every ten minutes to sweep the horizon for distress signals of the beaded lights of passing ships. Griff stood and plunged again, working out across the deepest part of the inlet in a slow trudgeon. A hundred yards out he came round in a slow circle, aimed for the flat rock, and ducked his head under for the leisurely return.

Better than halfway back he felt the sudden chill, like icy footsteps along his backbone. Something alive and very large was moving near him in the water.

A shark, he thought, and swam for the rock at full speed, surging out and rolling over, shaking seawater from his eyes and searching the placid gray surface for the triangular black fin. But he could see nothing and there was no sound but the *slup* of water under the rock. Imagination, he thought. Go ahead and swim in. It's close to midnight. It's cooler now and you can sleep.

Then it breached before his astonished eyes, wide and enormous in the gray light. He caught his breath and stared at the glistening black skin, whole square yards of it, while the water it displaced began rolling in to break in slow waves over the edge of his rock. Shark, hell. It was as big as a whale. It must be a whale that had entered the deep trench beyond the island and would follow it out again past Elephant's Back to reach the deeper water beyond the Spindle.

As though by prearrangement the high pale moon shone through a rift in the overcast and the sea surface glittered with silver light all the way to Beach Island. The vast bulk of whatever it was still moved past the rock where he stood. As long as a freight train, he thought with wonder, and just at that instant he saw the wound, a long gouge in the leathery flesh like a scar on the flank of a mountain.

Then it lifted its head and he saw that it was not a whale, nothing like anything that he had ever seen before, the sinuous neck rising slowly from the water twenty feet away while the bulk of the body was still sliding past—and then the head, larger than the head of a horse on a heroic statue, ugly as sin, covered with short spines like a sculpin, and turning slowly from side to side as if the creature were trying to get its bearings. It was still moving north through the channel when the great head slowly descended, and the dragon-like tail that must have been its means of locomotion stirred the final waves that came sloshing over the rock where he stood. Then it was gone.

He found that he was shaking from head to foot. His mouth was dry and his sight was bleary. Not from fear. Not even with cold, but with the sudden realization that a man can reach—a scientist, a poet—when he has at last put something together that was disparate before. When he understands clearly, as now, that it could not have been a capsized boat or a huge drifting log from the mouth of the Saco that tore the bottom out of that racing Sea Sled, but an honest-to-God sea serpent that at ten o'clock of a stormy morning had blundered up from the depths to the surface, that had then sunk broodingly down to the deep sea floor to wonder, if such creatures can be said to brood or wonder, what it had been that ploughed that bloody furrow in its back, and that now, close to the middle of the night, blind, groping, puzzled, had followed the channel inshore and out again, like a slow enormous locomotive on a curving track, disappearing as majestically and inexorably as it had come.

He glanced at the shore where his skiff lay high and dry at the edge of the beach grass. It would be possible to swim in, dash up the beach, untie the rope, grab the bow, swing it around, drag it to the water, unship the oars, and set off in pursuit. But the huge beast was already gone—half a mile away by now. And what if you caught up with it? What then?

Horsfield, he thought, peering up at the watchtower where Red about now would be yawning and stretching and getting up for yet another sweep with the big telescope all around the horizon from Wood Island Light on the north to Cape Porpoise ten miles down the coast.

Red Horsfield with his tales of bloody combat in North Africa. Horsfield with his deadpan yarns about everything under the sun. Horsfield topping every tall tale you ever used to tell with another twice as incredible. And now this—a story that would beat the wildest imagination in Horsfield's repertory, yet a story that, incredibly, was absolutely true.

So what now? he thought. He saw himself dashing into the wardroom at the station, breathless from running, dripping with seawater, bursting to tell them, midnight or not, of the sight he had seen, the adventure of a lifetime. Captain Staples would be nodding in the corner, Red Horsfield just coming down from his watch in the tower. And then what? *Listen! Listen to what I saw! Not a hundred yards offshore, following the Gut.*

What was it, Swiv? Tell us all about it.

I'll tell you, by God. It was a sea serpent, fifty feet long with a neck like a giraffe and a head like a nail keg and that gouge in its back from the Sea Sled this morning. That's what they hit. Don't you see how it all fits together?

Then he saw the faces—the gleam of rising doubt in Anton's beady eyes, followed by the slowly dawning tobacco-stained grin; Red Horsfield's pale eyebrows lifting like golden flags of disbelief and his big mouth widening to let out the bleat of incredulous laughter. For the love of God, now it's a sea serpent. There used to be a kid that told little ones like that one about the swimming deer off South Point that Harry Phillips said was nothing but a drifting tree root. And now here we've grown up to the biggest whopper of them all. A sea serpent, he says! Swiv, boy, it's late. Get along back home. Get yourself dried off, especially behind the ears. Roll into bed and pull up the covers and dream us up another nightmare.

It was no use. The biggest story he had ever had to tell would have to stay exactly where it was. Inside, hidden, and untold. Because there was not one single solitary soul who could ever back it up. A sea beast as long as the watchtower was high, and practically in your lap, and passing you like a slow freight, and not a chance in the world that anyone would ever believe that this was so.

He turned back to gaze out across the black and silver ocean, half-expecting to see the great head and the serpentine neck rising up once again above the surface. The white breakers were lashing away as always at the lava-like rock base of East Point. Against the northeast horizon the Spindle stood up like a bare mast. Somewhere out there the huge beast was swimming, deep down now and going deeper, heading towards or even back to the aboriginal hunting grounds from which the great storm had torn or persuaded it.

He was shivering still, but now with the cold. He swam ashore rapidly, limped across the stony beach to the sea grass, and slowly picked his way down the puddled gravel of the road towards the family cottage.

Then he heard the running footsteps and the voice calling his name. A shout—"Swiv! Hey, Swiv!"

Red Horsfield, hatless for once, his white shirt looming ghostlike in the half-light, was racing down the road from the station, racing so hard that his shoes skidded on the gravel when he stopped. "What in the hell was that?" he cried.

"What was what?"

"You know what I mean. That thing in the water."

"What did it look like?"

"In the telescope," Red panted. "I seen the whole thing. That black hide, acres of it. Then the damn long skinny neck and a head like a rain barrel and you on that rock right there looking at it and then the head coming down and going under and I lost it."

Griff was grinning now. "Take it easy," he said. "Just calm down. Show me. Point me out the place."

Horsfield gestured wildly. "Don't kid me, Griff. Right there in the Gut heading out for the Spindle."

"Now listen to me," Griff said. "I'm looking just where you're pointing and I've got pretty good eyes, but I tell you true, Swiv, Horsfield, I can't see one damn thing out there but moonshine."

Carlos Baker, renowned authority on Ernest Hemingway, has edited numerous literary texts, published a collection of short stories, poetry and three novels. He lives in New Jersey and is Woodrow Wilson Professor of Literature at Princeton University.

It's a case of intrigue!

FOREIGN intrigue and intrigue at home . . . there are intriguing stories to involve you in corners of the world you've never seen . . . or right at home in your own backyard or next door . . . in future issues of *Short Story International*.

Featured in the next issue of SSI

From England—*A Winter's Night Tale* by J.M. Scott.
A spellbinding exploration . . .

From Singapore—*Monster* by Catherine Lim.
Ironic and profound . . . an ancient bed fuels the feud between mother-in-law and daughter-in-law.

From Turkey—*Dog Tails* by Aziz Nesin.
A lesson in survival by a brilliant satirical humorist.

From South Africa—*The Old Boy* by Paul Dobson.
An insensitive, calculating "climber" and his former mentor are developed in counterpoint.

From Argentina—*The Rescue* by Daniel Moyano.
Suddenly caught in an extraordinarily tight spot, this woman's innate humanity surfaces.

From USA—*Behold the Key* by Bernard Malamud.
Trials of apartment hunting on a limited budget . . . in a foreign land.

And, for your reading pleasure, other intriguing, insightful stories from all lands.